Taking Off Her Rose Colored Glasses

by

P.L. John

Printed in the United States of America
ISBN:1-4392-5187-8
EAN13: 9781439251874
Library of Congress Control Number: 2009907593
Visit www.booksurge.com to order additional copies.

Dedication

To my children and their children
who have been my blessings in this life

Acknowledgments

A special thanks to my parents, Sue, Cousin Carol and Don
for their love and support.

My heartfelt thanks go to all who prayed on my behalf and
to those who offered a loving hug or a kind word.

And last but not least, to Crystal whose friendship and
expertise helped make this book a reality.

In memory of

My beloved beagle

"If you've ever had heartbreak, you know the heart never is cured, but you can heal it. And by healing it, you can relove….."

-   Kevin Cling

Chapter One

She sat on her cozy couch in the tiny apartment she now called home. Her reading glasses were perched precariously on the tip of her nose, her hair had been hastily pulled up in an untidy ponytail and her legs were tucked beside her leaving a small space at the crook of her knees for her beloved beagle Charlie to cuddle into. Although the volume was on low, the cheering from the excited contestants on the television game show could be heard playing in the background. Shelby didn't actually watch much TV anymore, but it was on anytime she was home. The noise it emitted was frequently the only sound that cut through the stillness in her life. She raised her dreamy eyes from the book she was reading and patted Charlie. She couldn't remember feeling so relaxed and content since the times she cuddled her sleeping babies in her arms. With a smile on her face, she laid her book down, let her head fall gently onto the back of the couch and fell to sleep.

* * *

Shelby took a moment to steady herself before she waltzed in through the front door of her house. With a slight stumble, she hurried up the stairway and slid discreetly into her bedroom. Her mother, who was standing at the kitchen stove busily finishing dinner, looked towards the stairway with questioning eyes. Louise never knew when Shelby would show up. When she did appear, she was usually evasive and moody. This had been a long and difficult year for the two of them. There was little friendship remaining between them and Louise would easily admit that she lost control of her youngest daughter years ago. But, this was Shelby's senior year in high school and as such, she would soon be turning eighteen. That meant Shelby would be free to move out of the house and choose the direction she wanted her life to continue in without any further interference from Louise or Levi. Not soon enough Louise thought as she shook her head.

Shelby locked her bedroom door with the old skeleton key that waited to be turned each time the door was shut. She flopped down on the edge of her bed, closed her dazed eyes and fell listlessly backwards. A sly smile lit her face and a quiet giggle broke out as she thought about the fun she and her friend Rylee had had after school. As she covered her mouth to smother the laugh, she grimaced from the pain she suddenly started to feel in her arm. There hadn't been any thought or concern that she might be paying for that good time with bruises and sore muscles while they were behaving so recklessly. They had been drinking that strawberry wine. It tasted terrible, but it was cheap and they couldn't be choosy.

Rylee had needed to drop her car off at the garage to get the oil changed after school so she had asked Neal if he would swing by and pick her and Shelby up at the garage. Neal was a couple years older than them, but he had always had a thing for Rylee so he was more than happy to oblige. He was also willing to buy them wine and drive the girls around for a while. Rylee had taken the front passenger seat and Shelby had hopped into the back seat so she too could be by a door. Every so often the two friends would shout out. "Fall out," and Neal would pull over to the side of the road and the girls would open their doors and fall out onto the ground, laughing hysterically. Shelby thought they had only done it a couple of times, but she could now see that her hip and arm were badly bruised. *Oh well*, she smiled, *it had been fun*. She slowly rolled over onto her stomach and decided to take a nap. She knew she had homework to do, but it could wait until study hall the next day.

Walking further and further away from the righteous path her parents had encouraged her to embrace, drinking or getting high was a daily event for Shelby now. She had always been a quiet and shy girl and as she entered her teenage years, she had desperately wanted to be part of the 'in' crowd. At that time in her life, the only way she knew how to accomplish that was to start partying like the group of kids she wanted to fit in with.

Her change in lifestyle made her feel as if she had attained the results she had so desired. Shelby felt very lucky that Rylee now hung out with her. Rylee was petite, pretty and popular. She came from a wealthy family and had been given a brand new sports car for her birthday. While Rylee was always involved in long term relationships with guys that adored her, Shelby had never really even been on an actual date. Oh, she had met up with guys at parties she went to, but that's where the relationship started and ended. She had had sex with more guys than she wanted to admit. Most of whom she really liked but, time after time when she would return to school on Monday following the parties, the guys she'd been with acted like they didn't even know her. At one particular party, Shelby had been elated that she had caught the attention of Nick whom she had had a crush on for almost a year. He had invited her inside the home of his friend, where the party was being held, on the pretence of watching Saturday Night Live with him. Shelby was flattered that he wanted to spend some time alone with her. Although she fully expected them to eventually have sex, the invitation to be alone together had given Shelby the impression that he was finally interested in her too. Maybe this was the opportunity she had been waiting for. A place and time for them to get to know each other better.

But, they didn't watch TV. They didn't even talk. With little fanfare, Nick had taken her straight to a bedroom, then coaxed the drunk and enamored Shelby into undressing and having fast and furious sex with him. As quickly as it started, it was over with. Nick rolled off Shelby, quickly got dressed and left her lying naked, alone and stunned in the dark room. The realization of what had just happened embarrassed Shelby. How could she have thought that Nick might actually be interested in her? She sat up and moved to the edge of the bed. The dim light coming in from the hallway enabled her to make out the lamp on the nightstand. She reached for it, turned it on and then gathered her clothes and dressed quickly. As she reached for her shoes, she noticed a pocket knife on the floor and knew it must have fallen out of Nick's pants pocket. She tucked it into the pocket of her jeans and quickly left the house. After searching through the vast rowdy crowd, she found Rylee and asked her if she minded if they left as she must have drank too much and she didn't feel well. As they left the party, Rylee was good enough not to ask any questions even though Shelby was pretty sure her friend knew what was going on. The following Monday, Shelby found Nick in the hall at school and handed the pocket knife to him. Although she didn't know what he would say or do, she didn't expect the coldness of him shrugging his shoulders, grabbing the knife and laughing as he turned and walked away with his buddies. Shelby stood there feeling numb and incredibly ashamed. It had happened again. Shelby had been rejected so often she started assuming she just wasn't good enough for a guy to have any real feelings for her.

The school year finally ended and graduation arrived. Shelby hated to admit it, but this was a big deal. She had always secretly loved school. It was one thing she had actually been good at. She had always had the ability to memorize well, so reading a chapter and answering the questions at the end or remembering formulas and equations had never been a problem. It was also in her nature to do a really good job at whatever task she was working on. Anytime she had an assignment it was done with precision and punctuality.

She remembered being in the seventh grade, handing in an assignment to the music theory teacher she had always feared but respected. The questions to the chapter were answered as accurately as if she had copied the answer word for word from the book, but she didn't copy it, she just remembered each word, the lives and works of the classical composers were so enthralling to her she couldn't wait for the next chapter.

Shelby was constantly struggling with her desire to be one of the popular kids and her ability and interest in school. She frequently wondered why she applied herself to this music class as with all her other classes. Classes were supposed to be stupid and teachers were supposed to be jerks. You were supposed to hate going to class and moan and groan because you had to be there. You certainly weren't supposed to enjoy them as she did. She wondered why she watched the filmstrips while many of the other girls were writing notes to each other and many of the boys were either sleeping or exploring the emerging breasts of the girls sitting next to them in the dark. It became evident that she wasn't doing something right. She wasn't on the receiving end of any of those notes and the boys weren't scampering to sit by her when the lights went out. She had felt so isolated and alone. She just wanted to be included, to have someone write a note to her or to have someone want to walk with her to her next class. Shelby decided that maybe if she started acting more like those other kids then maybe she'd be accepted by them. That had to be the answer and she had the perfect way to do it. Lee.

Shelby's brother Lee was four years older than her. She knew he was popular. He was good in sports, especially basketball and he always was doing something or another with this guy or that guy and he always had a girlfriend. She knew he smoked cigarettes, he'd been caught in school and his future in sports was shaky because of it. And she knew he drank. There were always beer cans in his bedroom and she heard him talk with his friends about it all the time. She got along with him okay; she just had to convince her parents to allow her to stay home weekends with him instead of going along with them to visit her grandmother. That's when he went to parties or even had them at their house. She had to be allowed. She'd be sick, that's it, and she couldn't go to grandmas as she was sick. She'd be okay, she wasn't a little girl, she babysat other families children all the time, she was responsible, she'd be fine, it was only for one night and Lee would be there anyway, don't worry.

She did it, they agreed. She realized that their reasoning was that they thought that Lee might actually act a little more responsibly if his little sister was there and that they never would have agreed if they knew Shelby was about to take that step into the life of alcohol, drugs and sex. And she did, in fact she not only took the first step, but she ran full speed.

Now, after years of unfulfilled dreams and the same feeling of emptiness she had five years earlier, Shelby had just received her diploma. Her brothers and older sister were sitting in the audience along with her parents. They looked proud of her. Maybe her parents were just relieved. In any case, they were there. After the ceremony they took pictures and went to a local restaurant for a nice meal. Shelby was glad that she had decided to wear the long white evening gown she had bought for this occasion. She had contemplated wearing some shorts and a tank top underneath the heavy white ankle length robe all the girls were required to wear to the ceremony. The guys robs were red and between the two, the school colors walked reverently down the aisle and across the stage. It was an honor to be wearing the traditional cap and gown, but it was an incredibly hot day and Shelby, as well as many of the other graduating seniors, had seriously considered wearing shorts instead of the formal wear. This definitely would have made it more cool and comfortable as they sat in the suffocating heat of the auditorium. But, as she sat around this table with all of her family, she felt refined, elegant, and very deserving of the honors that were being bestowed upon her today. Even though they were all a little uncomfortable with all this family togetherness, Shelby was really enjoying her day. She hadn't allowed her family into her life in years; in fact she had done just about everything she could to push them out. Her parents had tried in vain to calm her rebelliousness, but they had already fought that battle with Lee and lost, so they had finally given up in defeat. Instead, they concentrated their efforts on Shelby's older sister's failed marriage and doing what they could for the precious children from that marriage. They were also keeping Shelby's younger brother, a handsome and athletic boy, in their sights. Maybe things would go in the right direction with him. Shelby, realizing the miracle of this family gathering, looked around the table and smiled.

She couldn't really say she regretted the way she had lived her teenage years, in her mind and heart that was just the way it was. But she knew that her lifestyle hadn't helped her achieve her goal of becoming part of the gang any more than if she had remained that lonely student. All it did was open a door to a life where she wasn't feeling the loneliness because she was either drunk or high all the time. As it turns out, the girls she had struggled so many years to be friends with were planning on moving into an apartment together along with their boyfriends. They never considered asking Shelby to move in with them, they were moving on to the next phase of their lives and Shelby wasn't invited. Although there was a little sting of jealousy in Shelby's heart, she finally realized that she didn't fit into Rylee's life now any more than she ever had. Shelby had been reliable, someone you knew you could count on to be available to go someplace or do something with. The substance and sincerity of the friendship was an illusion. Shelby had fought for and held on to something that wasn't even there.

Shelby hadn't enrolled in college and she wasn't exactly sure what she would be doing after that day or where her future would lead. She only knew that she had done enough partying to last her a life time. Yes, she was definitely sick of all the drinking and drugs. She was sick of waking up after yet another party remembering who'd she'd been a sexual conquest to this time. She was sick of it all. She'd party hearty'd throughout her teenage years, but now at the ripe old age of eighteen she decided that wasn't the type of life she wanted anymore. The more she thought about it, the more sense it made that the best thing to do was to leave the area. Shelby decided to call Diane, a girl she graduated with who had talked about moving away from the area. They got together and by the time their conversation was over, Shelby and Diane decided to move to Florida.

Shelby remembered that a cousin of hers had worked at Disney World at one time and she knew that her brother Lee had lived in that area working as a bellboy at a hotel. So, they figured it was someplace they could go, find jobs and make a living. The decision felt right and Shelby was eagerly anticipating taking this next step in her life. They decided to leave after the first of the year. That would give each of them time to earn some money to put it aside for the trip. When Shelby told her parents about her plans, they were excited for her and even bought her some luggage. Shelby couldn't help but smile about that. Even though she had already moved out of their home into an apartment she wondered whether they were a little relieved she was moving away.

* * *

Chapter Two

Since right after she finished high school, Shelby had been working at the bowling alley as a waitress. It wasn't her dream job and she really didn't know if she'd ever really gotten the hang of it but, it was work and she was leaving in a little over a month anyway. She found that carrying a tray with bottles and glasses filled to the brim with beverages was a lot harder than she thought it would be. She was slow and cautious because anytime she rushed, half of the contents of the glasses ended up on her tray. Fortunately she hadn't tipped over any beer bottles or spilt a drink on a customer yet. All she knew was that now she certainly had a better appreciation for the balancing act waitresses performed.

Shelby realized that most of the men on the leagues were extremely serious about bowling and were very competitive with each other. But there were obviously others that just enjoyed the game or simply wanted an evening out with the guys. Between the naked women on the back of the deck of cards they held in one hand and the beer held tightly in the other hand, some men seemed to be more interested in the camaraderie of their fellow team mates than what was happening on the lanes. This party atmosphere with all the hoots, hollers and cheers made it a fun place to work at anyway. Yes, occasionally someone would overindulge in their alcohol consumption and become obnoxious and annoying, but for the most part the teams were only there for about two hours, only enough time to start catching a good buzz.

The men in the bar area were a different crowd altogether. They were there to get drunk and to try and fill the emptiness they were dealing with in their lives. Shelby had been on that side of the bar with a fake ID for too many years and now knew that the answer to problems couldn't be found with booze. She also knew she didn't want to be part of that empty life any more. Therefore, these were the men Shelby stayed clear of. From past encounters, she discovered that they were usually under the delusion that she would be willing to help them fill whatever void they were trying to fill by jumping into the backseat of their cars with them. She never encouraged these advances and had no desire to be a part of their delusions but, it always seemed that the more they drank the more aggressive and confident in their prowling ability they became. She had received plenty of propositions and found that the quickest way to waylay these advances was to smile and tell them that she didn't fall in love that easy when they suggested she leave with them and go fall in love.

Shelby hadn't had a sexual relationship in months. It was amazing how less persuasive men could be when you weren't drunk. She now found herself wondering what the intrigue was with those encounters. Not only was there no emotional fulfillment for her, she couldn't even think of any bed partner she'd had that was worth remembering let alone worth looking forward to a second go round with.

While Shelby was working one cold November night, Diane stopped in. As they began talking, Diane mentioned that some of the gang they graduated with was getting together later that night at Mark's place to play Euchre. She asked Shelby if she wanted to come join them. Since Shelby didn't go out much anymore, she thought that sounded like it might be fun. Playing cards was something they used to do every day in the senior center her last year of high school and she hadn't played since then. Diane promised to be by at about 11:00 to pick her up. That would give Shelby time to clean up the tables after the leagues were over with.

As promised, Diane stopped by shortly after Shelby had finished wiping down the tables. It had been a busy night. Not only were there bowling leagues but due to it being so close to Thanksgiving, there were people in town visiting for the holidays. Shelby was more than ready to get off her feet.

They arrived at the trailer where there were about ten people laughing and holding cards. Some were at the kitchen table, some were sitting on the couch and the rest were on the floor gathered around an old coffee table. Mark and another guy Shelby didn't know were sitting on the couch. Mark gestured for Diane and Shelby to come on in and then they scooted over to make room for them to sit down. After taking off her coat and sitting down, Shelby looked around and had to smile. You could tell that guys were living here, there were only a few pieces of worn furniture, the sink had dirty dishes in it and there were beer tabs strung together, hanging on the walls. Shelby's attention shifted back to the card game as the next hand was dealt.

What fun they all seemed to be having. Laughing, telling stories from school and talking about the big plans for everyone's future. Diane mentioned that it was hard to believe that Thanksgiving was only a few days away, that Christmas was right around the corner and that she and Shelby would be leaving for Florida right after January first. Everyone was excited for them, and that excitement seemed to carry throughout the night. Although some of the people had left to go home, Shelby and Diane were still laughing and playing cards with Mark and his friend Todd when Todd turned to look up at the clock.

"I didn't know it was so late," Todd said as he was getting up off the couch. "I have to get going so I can be in the woods when the sun comes up."

Diane laughed. "Why do you have to be in the woods?"

"To go hunting, what do you think?"

Diane got up to carry some of the beer cans to the garbage and said. "I forgot it was deer season, hey good luck."

Shelby smiled. "I can't believe it's so late. You ready to give me a ride home Diane?"

Todd smiled mischievously. "Hey, why don't you come hunting with me?"

Shelby didn't know Todd well enough to know whether he was joking or not so instead of guessing wrong and embarrassing herself she replied in a surprised and questioning tone. "Me?"

Todd looked more serious when he said. "Yeah, you ever been hunting?"

Shelby thought that he might as well have asked her if she'd ever walked on the moon because that would have been as unimaginable to her as the thought of her father or brothers inviting her to spend a day hunting with them. She must have had a confused look on her face as she simply said. "No."

Todd looked nervously down at the ground momentarily then he shifted his stance from one foot to the other. He raised his head and Shelby noticed the smile was gone. His questioning eyes looked into hers and in a soft voice he said. "It's great walking in the woods. I'm leaving in a few minutes. Um, why don't you come along?"

Shelby could feel his nervousness and apprehension as if he expected her to reject his invitation and that's when she knew he really wanted her to come along with him.

Diane laughed at her hesitation. "Go ahead, and then I can go straight home and go to bed."

As Shelby looked into Todd's dark pleading eyes, she was drawn to him instantly and knew she wanted to go with him. She smiled shyly and said. "Okay, if you really want me to tag along."

"Sure, come on let's go."

She exhaled heavily as she couldn't believe what she had just agreed to do, but she was also smiling. Shelby and Diane said their good-byes as did Mark and Todd. Diane took off down the road in her car and Shelby got into the passenger seat of Todd's car. During the drive from Mark's trailer on the outskirts of the village to the rural wooded area where they would be hunting, Shelby sat in excited astonishment as she thought about everything that had happened since Diane stopped in to see her at the bowling alley early yesterday evening.

This was all so unexpected. Shelby had certainly noticed Todd while they were playing cards, and she had been attracted to him. Not only was he very good looking but he had a raw maleness about him that pulled at her. Even though she had noticed him looking at her a couple times, he really didn't give any hint that he was interested in her. And now, here they were, going to spend more time together.

They drove down an old dirt road and turned onto a long driveway that had a cabin at the end. Todd parked the car, turned to Shelby and smiled.

"Are you ready?"

Shelby nervously shrugged her shoulders. "I guess."

Todd got his gun out of the trunk and then with enthusiasm and excitement said. "Okay then, let's go."

Shelby hesitantly said. "Aren't you supposed to wear something red or orange or something like that?"

Todd laughed. "Yeah, but these are private woods and there shouldn't be any city hunters near that will shoot at us."

Shelby smiled weakly. "Okay."

They started into the woods. Shelby couldn't believe she was doing this. While she was trying to concentrate on not tripping over a branch and making a fool of herself, it was impossible not to look around and admire the beauty and majesty that surrounded them. The leaves had already fallen from their branches and scattered on the ground along with traces of snow that remained here deep in the woods from the snowfall they received several days earlier. The sun had only risen about a half hour earlier and the fingers of sunlight were starting to stream through the branches that had been stripped bare of their leaves. It was quiet, no, that wasn't the right description, it was peaceful here. Todd led them through the woods for what seemed like forever. Shelby could tell that he was comfortable in the woods. He walked with such authority that she knew he had walked this path many times. Shelby had to admit she was impressed, she felt like she was being led by an expert in tracking. Then Todd stopped abruptly. Shelby caught up and looked ahead. They were at the edge of a small open field and in the middle of the field was a lone maple tree, with low hanging branches.

"This is my favorite spot to sit."

Shelby noticed that he had a wistful look on his face and a gleam in his eyes that made it clear to her that what he was saying was the truth.

Todd looked at her and smiled. "Come on, we're climbing that tree."

Shelby knew she must have had a stunned look on her face but what was she supposed to do? She hadn't climbed a tree since she was a child climbing the pine trees in her grandmother's front yard. She nodded and they walked to the tree.

"Step into my hand and I'll boost you up onto that first branch, then I'll climb up to the next one up."

Shelby nodded, took a deep breath and stepped towards his clasped hands. *I can Do this, I Can do this, oh God, I'm not that light, what if he can't handle my weight and I fall on my ass? God, I Can't do this!*

"Come on."

She nodded her head and stepped up. She raised and somehow got her foot in the crook of the branch, grabbed onto the trunk and pulled herself up. Moments later, to her amazement, she was sitting where she was supposed to be. There was a second branch close to the one she was on so she scooted over so she was sitting comfortably between the branches.

Shelby felt such a relief, she had made it through the woods and up into the tree without incident. All her penned up nervousness and fear seemed to evaporate. She suddenly felt giddy and giggled as she looked down at him. "You're turn."

He lifted his gun and placed it on a level area between two branches, then he jumped and grabbed hold of another branch on the other side of the tree. Half climbing and half using the strength in his arms, Todd pulled himself up onto the branch that was above her.

Whoa, Shelby was taken aback. If she thought she was impressed with his ability to find his way through the woods, she was doubly impressed with the shear strength he had. He had lifted her with ease to her branch and then pulled himself onto a higher branch swiftly and easily. She hadn't noticed whether he was muscular or not the night before, but now she could envision the well toned muscles under his heavy winter coat.

Once he was settled on his branch he looked at her. "Now you have to be quiet. Just sit still okay?"

Shelby shut off her thoughts of Todd's muscular arms and nodded.

They stayed in the tree for hours. Shelby could see why Todd enjoyed the woods and especially this tree. It was peaceful and beautiful. Shelby was relaxed and soon realized that the long night was quickly catching up with her. She was afraid she was going to fall asleep. Suddenly, on the other side of the field there was a rustle and Shelby noticed Todd raising his gun. A deer appeared, walking slowly and cautiously. Shelby was so excited. It was the first deer she had ever seen that wasn't mounted to a wall.

She yelled. "Oh look, there's a deer."

The deer picked its head up, looked in their direction, and then quickly ran back into the woods.

Todd was exasperated and as he lowered the barrel of his gun he said. "I thought I told you to be quiet?"

Shelby realized what she had done and was embarrassed by her outburst. Her eyes were still wide with surprise as she raised her hand to cover her mouth. "Oh, I'm sorry. It's the first deer I've ever seen, I didn't mean to yell."

Todd looked down at her with scolding eyes, shook his head in disbelief then smiled. "That's okay I have other days to hunt." He laughed as he said. "Since you've probably scared everything away that was within a mile of here, we might as well head out."

He jumped down from the branch and held out his arms to help Shelby get down. Shelby was so tired she didn't really even care if she fell getting out of the tree. She tried to lift herself from the branches but she wasn't moving. She tried again, but again she didn't move and with a feeling of dread she looked at Todd.

"I'm stuck."

Shelby was mortified, her face was red with embarrassment and she thought she might start crying. Her stupid wide hips had gotten wedged between the two branches and she wasn't moving.

Todd burst out laughing. "See if I ever take you hunting again." His eyes were warm and his smile made her able to laugh herself. "Just drop your legs between the branches and I'll lower you down that way."

Shelby did as she was told and started to drop to the ground. Todd grabbed her around the waist and eased her down. After her feet touched the ground, she stood there in his arms, pressed close to him, and this time she could feel the strength of his arms through the jacket. She looked into his warm, smiling eyes and felt her heart skip a beat. Shelby pulled out of his arms and Todd took a step back. They were both silent and she wondered if he had felt the pull towards her that she was feeling for him.

It seemed to take both of them a minute to gather their wits about them, then Todd said softly. "Come on, let's go."

Their walk back to the car was slower and he seemed to be walking beside her now instead of charging ahead of her like before. He offered his hand when crossing a fallen tree trunk and all too quickly they were in the car heading back down the hill.

* * *

Chapter Three

Todd dropped Shelby off at the curb in front of her apartment building and as she opened the car door she turned and looked at him.

"Thanks for taking me hunting with you today and I'm sorry I scared the deer away," she said apologetically and with a hint of embarrassment. "I can see why you like it in the woods, it's very peaceful there."

When Todd smiled at her, Shelby felt a tug at her heart. She looked into his dark eyes that sparkled with both amusement and warmth. He had a mustache but she could tell that he had a crooked smile, almost like there was a smirk on his lips. With his dark hair that touched the collar of his coat, she thought he looked rugged and handsome.

"That's okay. You look tired."

"Yeah, I really am. Thanks again." Shelby started to get out of the car when she felt Todd gently tug on her arm to stop her from exiting the car. The hold on her arm, though gentle, startled her and she turned back towards him wondering what she might have forgotten.

"Hey wait a minute," he said quickly. "You doing anything later?"

Shelby was as dumbfounded now as she had been with the earlier invitation to go hunting with Todd. She hadn't been expecting this either.

"No," she said slowly, uncertain of what was happening. "I'm just hanging around watching TV tonight; I'm saving money for my trip."

"Oh, that's right. Well I might be in town later. Would you mind if I stopped by to say hi?"

Shelby felt her jaw drop and her heart skip a beat at the same time. *Come on; don't just sit there with your mouth open, answer him.* "Yeah, sure," she finally managed to choke out around the lump in her throat.

"Okay," Todd said with a quick and easy smile. "See you later."

Shelby ran up the stairs to her second floor apartment. Her heart was racing and her hands were shaking. She stood in front of her apartment door trying to calm down so that she could unlock it. She took a deep breath and laid her forehead on the door and stood there thinking. *What did you say ok for? He's not any different than any of the other guys you've known, he only wants to go to bed with you and you all but invited him to.* She shook her head, unlocked the door and went into her apartment. After locking back up she started to head to the kitchen to grab something quick to eat but realized she wasn't hungry. So instead, she just turned into her bedroom, took off her clothes and plopped down on her bed. She was completely exhausted and went to sleep quickly. But just before she did, she closed her eyes and remembered the moment when she was in Todd's arms. She could feel his muscular arms around her and feel her body heat up from his closeness. Shelby knew she was in trouble.

After her long nap, Shelby climbed out of bed and went to her small, dreary kitchen to get something to eat. The cupboards held only a minimal amount of eating utensils and cookware and there wasn't much left to eat in the refrigerator either. There was only a jar of jam that was almost empty, a bottle of ketchup, half a carton of eggs and a few cans of Pepsi left besides the leftovers from dinner a couple of days earlier. She couldn't put off going to the store much longer but grocery shopping was such a pain. Bundling up and walking to the store, then having to carry the bags of groceries back and lug them up to her second floor apartment wasn't fun at all. She pulled out the left over pork chop and sat at the wobbly little table she'd found at a yard sale. She ate the pork chop cold and let her mind wander to the previous night. The whole night had been fun. She couldn't remember the last time she had truly enjoyed herself like that. Although some of the guys had been drinking beer, it wasn't like the parties she'd gone to throughout her teenage years where the sole purpose of drinking had been to get plastered and pass out. Last night had been different. It had just been fun playing cards, talking, laughing and reminiscing. And she had been included. She'd felt welcome and had finally been treated with kindness instead of like a body without a face or name.

Then she thought about her morning hunting excursion. If Todd realized that the trip to the woods had been the first time she was ever invited to just hang out and go someplace with a guy, he would probably think she was pretty pathetic. Regardless of that, she had a wonderful time. But, was it hunting and walking in the woods that she enjoyed? Or had it been the time that she had spent with Todd? Maybe it was both. It didn't matter, she would be leaving for Florida soon and if she was honest with herself she'd admit that she probably wouldn't ever see him again anyway. No sense making more out of it than there was.

Shelby shook her head to try and dispel her feelings of enjoyment at being asked and included in such a good time. She hopped in the shower to ward off any more deep thoughts. She'd barely gotten out and was still drying off when the phone rang. It was Diane.

"Hi Shelby, I just wanted to make sure you made it home okay."

"Yeah, we spent a few hours in the woods and I was home before noon."

Diane's voice changed from one of concern to one of curiosity and excitement. "Well come on, tell me everything that happened."

Shelby tried to sound nonchalant but the happiness in her voice gave her away as she told Diane everything that happened that morning and that Todd had mentioned he might stop by later.

"Does that surprise you?" Diane said emphatically. "Didn't you notice the way he was checking you out all night long?"

Shelby laughed nervously. "No, you must have been seeing things. How much did you drink?"

"I wasn't seeing things; he was looking at you as much as he was looking at his cards. I think you'll be seeing a lot of him."

After she hung up the phone, Shelby tried to shrug off Diane's suggestion that Todd was interested in her but; she couldn't help feeling a little elated about what Diane had said. Shelby had felt that the attraction between Todd and her had been mutual, but then again, she really didn't trust her perception of how guys felt about her. In the past, it never failed that every time she had thought a guy was as interested in her as she was in him, she would discover that they were just taking advantage of her serious crush on them to score with her in bed.

Todd was definitely good looking and his warm eyes and smile had started to melt her heart. Shelby just wasn't sure whether her heart was playing tricks on her again. She also had to admit that the thought of his lean, muscular body heated parts of her that had nothing to do with the emotional feeling of her heart. She longed to be held in those strong arms again…

She shook her head. *What are you thinking? First of all you're never going to see him again and second of all you're just falling back into the same old routine with guys. You're supposed to be changing, growing up, and maturing.*

But it wasn't the same and she knew it. When they had been in each others arms and had looked into each others eyes, it had been something different, something entirely new. Shelby had felt and seen the desire he had for her, yet, unlike all her previous experiences, he hadn't pushed it any further. He hadn't taken advantage of her even though she knew he could have convinced her to let him come up to her apartment without a fight when he had dropped her off earlier. She had never experienced that before, a guy basically turning down a sure thing.

Shelby's lack of self worth suddenly reared its ugly head. Was it possible she had read him wrong? Maybe he wasn't even attracted to her. Maybe that's why he didn't want to come up to her apartment. Suddenly as depressed as she'd previously been excited, Shelby turned on the TV and went to sit on the old brown velour couch that had been in the apartment when she moved in. If she remembered right, there was supposed to be a good movie on and since she'd slept most of the day, she was wide awake and desperately needing a break from her ricocheting thoughts. She wasn't going to analyze things any more, she was just going to sit and watch the movie.

She was a sucker for romance movies and this western with the lonesome desperado and the woman who had captured his heart was drawing all of her attention. She was so engrossed in the show that when her doorbell rang and Shelby glanced at the clock, she was surprised to see that an entire hour had slipped by. She rose and assuming it was Diane, flung the door open, only to find a somewhat nervous looking Todd on her doorstep.

"Hi, I told you I might be in town tonight. You don't mind me stopping by do you?" he asked with a sheepishly innocent look on his face.

Shelby was flabbergasted, she never thought he would actually stop by to see her and she stuttered. "No, no come on in."

She opened the door and stepped back to let him pass. She didn't know what to do or say. Todd must have seen that she too felt awkward and nervous as he smiled. This simple gesture put Shelby at ease.

"You don't have to worry about your boots," she said when he gestured toward his boots and looked at her questioningly. "Come on in."

He started to take off his coat and Shelby walked over to him. "Here, I'll take that." She took his coat and draped it over the back of the chair that held her 12" black & white TV on its scarred wood seat. Bedsides her couch, the straight back chair was the only other piece of furniture she had in her living room.

After they sat on the couch, Shelby became very self-conscious as she noticed Todd had on a nice pullover shirt and corduroy pants whereas she was in a pair of worn jeans and an old t-shirt. She was barefoot and didn't have any make-up on. Boy, was she making a good impression or what? She never thought Todd would actually stop by and therefore hadn't done anything to prepare herself for company, especially male company.

Little did she know that Todd thought she was just as attractive without makeup as she had been with it on. She was unpretentious and had a warmth and simplicity about her that drew him in and made him feel comfortable. The fact that she didn't appear to have remembered he had said he'd stop by, or expected him to, somehow made her all the more appealing to him. When he had seen her come into the trailer the evening before, he had noticed that she looked uneasy, like she didn't know what to expect as she walked in the door. He saw a hint of fear and a shyness that made his heart go out to her. He suddenly felt very protective of this girl he hadn't even met yet and wanted to make her feel at ease. He'd told Mark to move over and make room for the two girls that had just come in. Throughout the evening, he found himself doing and saying what he could to make her feel at ease and welcome.

"I was just watching a movie on TV; would you like to watch something else?" Shelby asked as she stood up nervously.

"No, that's alright, keep it on whatever you were watching," he said in an effort to calm her.

"Okay," she agreed softly and sat back down. "I don't have anything good to eat and I don't have any beer but I have some Pepsi in the refrigerator if you want one," she said rapidly, all in one breath, her eyes wide and vulnerable.

"Yeah, that'd be good."

"I'll be right back."

Shelby jumped to her feet and Todd watched her as she hurried away. She was tall and thin, her long blond hair swayed gently as she walked. Her hips were gently curved from a waist that seemed to call out to him to wrap his arms around it, and her feet were bare which only enhanced her appeal.

As she disappeared into a doorway; Todd sat back and remembered how Mark had described her when they saw each other earlier in the evening. He said she had always been shy even though she was pretty much a party girl up until earlier that year when she all but dropped out of sight. She had finished her senior year of high school at the end of the first semester as she had loaded up on her classes and had enough credits to graduate. Shortly after that she had gotten a job and moved into her own place. He also said she'd been very popular and there were a few guys he knew that had wanted to ask her out because they thought she was so nice and good looking but they didn't because they were a little intimidated. She seemed to gravitate towards the guys that strutted down the halls at school with a different girl hanging from their arm every week and whose lives revolved around the weekend and the next party.

Before their conversation had been interrupted by dinner, Mark had remarked that there were a lot of people who wondered why she hung out with guys that treated girls like they were disposable.

Todd leaned his head back on the couch and thought about all of this as he anxiously waited for Shelby to return. He wanted her to be there, by his side.

Shelby walked towards the kitchen but turned into the bathroom first. She closed the door and sheepishly looked into the mirror. *God, I look terrible, my hair is still wet, I look half-dead because I don't have any make-up on and I have these scrubby clothes on. Oh well, if I change my clothes now he'll know I did it just because he's here, but I'm going to at least put some mascara on.* Shelby grabbed her make-up bag, pulled out the tube of mascara and willed her hands to stop shaking so she could put it on her eyelashes. She also dabbed a little blush onto her cheeks and then ran a brush through her long hair. At least she could look halfway decent for him.

Shelby came out of the bathroom, continued on to the kitchen and grabbed two cans of pop. When she came back to the living room, Todd was leaning his head back on the couch; he had his right arm on the armrest of the couch and was sitting with his left ankle resting on the knee of the opposite leg. He looked a little nervous himself. That thought helped Shelby relax a bit as she handed the can of Pepsi to him before sitting back down at the other end of the couch. She would have liked to be snuggled right next to him but maybe the fact that he was an arm length away was a good idea.

"So, what were you in town for tonight?"

"Uh, I went over to Mark's mothers' house for dinner, she's a pretty good cook and it's nice getting a home cooked meal once in a while."

Shelby nodded, thinking of the single pork chop she'd eaten for dinner and then said. "So, you're good friends with Mark huh? Do you live in that trailer too?"

"Yeah, Mark and I are good friends, he went to school here and I went to another school, but we've grown up together," Todd rambled nervously. "I almost think of him as my brother and his mom treats me like I'm a member of his family. I was pretty interested in his older sister at one time and even figured I would have liked to marry her someday but then she ran off an eloped with the guy she's married to now. Goes to show you how farfetched that idea was huh?" Todd laughed embarrassingly. "Her husband and I are good friends too, either he didn't know how I felt about her or he realized I didn't have a chance with her. And no, I don't live in the trailer with Mark. For the last few months, I've been staying with Kyle, who's a friend of my brother-in-law. He has an apartment and needed a roommate to help with expenses and I needed a place to live so it worked out pretty good. I don't know how long I'll stay there, but its okay for now."

There was a long silence between them then. Shelby thought about what Todd had said and didn't quite know how she felt about it. It was Todd's idea to stop by and see her and everything seemed to be going really great between them, so why had he just mentioned that he'd had some really serious feelings for his friend's sister? Although he implied it was all in the past and even seemed to joke about it like it had been the crush of a young boy, Shelby didn't know what she was supposed to say to this.

As soon as it was out of his mouth, Todd realized that he had said something that he probably shouldn't have mentioned. So, instead of taking the chance that he'd nervously blurt out something else that he hadn't meant to, he quickly said.

"Hey, your movies back on. Do you mind if we just sit here and finish watching it? It looks like its pretty good."

Relieved, Shelby smiled at Todd, nodded her head and turned to look at the TV. She decided that it was silly to think about or worry about something so minor. So what if he had fallen for this girl, nothing came out of it and she married another guy. Shelby admitted to herself that she had fallen for a number of guys and thought they were 'the one' so she stopped worrying about all that and concentrated on the here and now.

She was admittedly a bundle of nerves and at first couldn't even hear what the characters were saying on TV. She heard the noise, but all she could think about was Todd sitting there. He really was handsome and so nice and he was here, in her apartment, on her couch, watching TV with her. Eventually she began to feel more relaxed, so she snuggled into her corner of the couch and became absorbed in the events of the movie.

It seemed like they had just started watching the movie together and all of a sudden it was over. Shelby was a little teary eyed, the ending was sad. When she realized how foolish she must look, she took a deep breath and laughed.

"Well, that movie was pretty stupid wasn't it?"

Before Shelby had pulled her tears back, Todd had already noticed that she was getting pretty choked up. He could read the emotion on her face just like he could read it when she had walked into the door of the trailer. He wanted to put his arm around her, pull her towards him and just hold her tightly to sooth her. But he thought maybe she'd think he was putting the moves on her too soon, so he kept his arm at his side.

"Nah, it was okay." He stood up and looked at her. "It's getting pretty late; I'd better let you get some sleep. Uh, do you have to work tomorrow night?"

"Yeah, but the leagues get done at 9:00 so it will be an early night."

"Well then, would you like to go uptown after you're done and get a hamburger or pizza?"

Completely delighted with the invitation, Shelby smiled. "Sure that would be great."

"Okay, I'll see you tomorrow then?"

"Yeah."

As if being unable to contain himself any longer, Todd stepped towards Shelby, gently grasped her upper arms and kissed her. The kiss was soft and sweet and there was a hesitation, as if he were waiting to see if she would kiss him back.

He didn't have to worry whether the kiss would be returned or not as it was exactly what she wanted. She kissed him and it was heavenly. As Todd's arms encircled Shelby's waist, her arms slid easily around his neck. They held each other close and the kiss deepened. She became light headed and her knees felt as though they were about to buckle. The strength of his embrace and the sweetness of his kiss shook Shelby to her very core. She held onto Todd tightly so she wouldn't lose her balance. Never before had she experienced a kiss that left her so breathless and shaky. As they pulled away from each other, Shelby could see by the look in Todd's eyes that he had felt the effects of their kiss just as much as she had.

She didn't know what to expect next. Would he try to convince her to let him stay the night? She knew she wouldn't tell him no as she was flushed with heat and desire. But he simply looked at her, smiled and took a step back.

"I'd better get going, I'll see you tomorrow, okay?"

Shelby smiled back and nodded her head. "Okay."

She stepped back into her apartment and watched him go down the stairway. When he got to the bottom he turned around, looked up at her and gave her a quick smile and a wave goodbye.

After Shelby closed and locked the door, she leaned back against it and closed her eyes. She was still breathless, her heart was racing and she couldn't help but smile. This was the first time that a guy had ever asked her on a real date, it was the first time she had ever spent an evening alone with a guy just sitting and watching TV and it was the first time the guy she was with hadn't expected her to have sex with him.

* * *

Chapter Four

There was a spring in Shelby's step and a smile on her face that couldn't be shaken from her no matter how obnoxious and surly the customers were at the bowling alley the following night while she was working. The equipment on lane ten had jammed. The two teams that were on lanes nine and ten were delayed for almost a half hour while the equipment was being repaired. This delay had aggravated a few of the team members and they were insistent that the owner of the bowling alley supply their drinks while they waited. Shelby had a hard time convincing them that they would have to discuss that with him themselves after he returned from working on the machinery.

Although she and Todd hadn't done anything exciting, Shelby had had the most wonderful night in her life the previous night. Shelby brought her fingers to her lips and smiled as she remembered the kiss that not only heated her body, but had also melted her heart.

The leagues were almost finished and Shelby was excited and filled with anticipation about going out with Todd soon. For some reason she didn't even question whether he would be there, there seemed to be something unspoken yet understood between them. Neither of them felt the need to play games with each other's hearts.

As she was wiping down the tables, Shelby stopped and slowly turned around. She felt his presence. It wasn't the eerie feeling of being watched, it was a warm feeling of a kindred spirit or a soul mate. She knew Todd was there.

He stood there smiling. Little did she know that he had been in the bar for the last fifteen minutes watching her as she went about the chore of cleaning off the tables and wiping them down. Throughout the time she had a smile on her face and Todd could have sworn she was humming along with the song on the stereo system. Her long blond hair had been pulled back into a ponytail while she had been waiting on the customers, but now she had let it loose and it was covering her face as she leaned over to wipe the last table. He had a strong desire to gently tuck the long strands of hair behind her ear just so he could continue to see her smile. He wanted to run his hands through her hair and to kiss those luscious lips. As he walked out towards the lanes to where Shelby stood, his heart quickened. What was it about this girl that made him feel this way?

Shelby's smile became even brighter. "You timed that perfectly, I just finished up. Let me take care of this stuff and change my clothes and I'll be ready."

"Sure, take your time." Todd tucked his hands into his pockets and leaned against the snack bar. He tried not to look anxious and excited as he felt.

Shelby quickly rinsed out the dishrag, hung it over the edge of the sink and put away the bottle of spray cleaner she had been using. That chore finished, she went into the women's restroom to clean herself up. She had brought a washcloth and change of clothing to work with her. After she washed her face and hands, she put on some fresh make-up that she had thrown in her purse. She never wore much, just some mascara and blush, but tonight she put on some eye shadow and lip-gloss too. After she changed into her clean clothes she looked into the mirror. She knew she wasn't the most beautiful woman in the world, her face had some flaws that she wished she had the money to change, and she also weighed a little more than she would have wanted to, but she knew this was as good as it got and she felt she at least looked attractive.

As Shelby came out of the bathroom, Todd couldn't help but stare at her and thank the lucky stars for his fate in meeting her. She had changed into a pair of faded straight legged jeans and a button up blouse that was a soft shade of pink. He thought she was lovely, almost angelic with her long blond hair swinging as she walked, the light in her eyes and the smile that warmed his heart. She was tall with long legs and shapely hips and all he could think about was how much he wished she were in his arms again.

"Ready?" He asked as he reached for her hand with his.

"Yeah, where are we going to go?" she replied as she slipped her hand into his.

"It's kind of late to go uptown, why don't we just go up the street and have a hamburger?"

"That sounds good to me, let's go." Shelby turned towards the door that exited the bowling alley through the lanes area instead of through the bar area. She knew what to expect from the patrons in the bar. There would be cat calls and hoots along with fists pumping in the air in celebration of Todd's victory in scoring with Shelby. It was possible that Todd would revel in the attention, but Shelby didn't want anything to do with that room full of testosterone.

They left and got in Todd's car. Shelby sat back for the short ride up the street. The truck stop was a diner where the townsmen met for coffee every day to discuss world events or just gossip. Families came there for its good cooking and friendly staff. It was close to the expressway so there was its share of truckers that stopped in as well. Best of all, it was open all night so you never had to worry about where to go if you wanted to get something to eat after the conventional dinner hour.

They found a nice table in a quiet corner and looked over the menu. Todd was thinking that if Shelby was anything like him, she hadn't eaten much that day and was hungry. He didn't want her to think she just had to order a small hamburger so he suggested that the hoagies sounded good.

"I was thinking they sounded good too," she agreed with a smile.

So Todd ordered them each a hoagie with everything, an order of french fries and a Pepsi for them both.

"You know, I used to work at a bowling alley before I got this job working security and I liked it."

"Oh yeah, what did you do?"

"I worked in back of the lanes with the machines. I reset the bowling pins and basically fixed any problems with the machines."

"How come you switched to working security?"

"I guess I just kind of fell into it. My Uncle Chris and Aunt Mary manage the campgrounds where I work. A security guard position became available so I took the job. Being the new guy, I usually get the night and weekend shifts. It interfered with the hours I was working at the bowling alley so I had to quit that job."

"Do you like working security and are you glad you made the change?"

"Yeah, in fact I'm even starting to think that maybe I'd like to become a police officer." He hesitated before admitting. "My friends think I'm crazy."

"If you feel that strongly about wanting to do it, I think you should go ahead and give it a try." He watched in delight as her face colored and she quickly added. "Besides you'd look good in a uniform."

Todd smiled beneath his mustache with that wicked sideways sneer that looked positively devilish. The smile reached his dark eyes, making them bright and sparkling.

"I give you credit," she went on. "I've never had a clear idea of what I wanted to do for a career. I know I like kids and have always wanted to be a mother but, I just could never figure out what kind of job I wanted. I know it's not being a waitress in a bowling alley." They both laughed. "That's part of the reason I decided to move to Florida. I might find something interesting to do down there."

Todd nodded but the smile wasn't as bright on his face as it had been. The thought of Shelby leaving when they had just met didn't seem fair and it was hard for him to pretend he was really happy about it.

Just then, their meals were brought to them and all serious thoughts left their minds as they greedily ate the delicious hoagies. They made small talk and smiled throughout the meal.

"That was good, I was really hungry." Todd said as he took the last sip of his Pepsi.

"I was too and that hoagie was good, but I sure am full now." Shelby patted her stomach to emphasize.

They got up from the table and Todd gestured for Shelby to go ahead as they weaved through the narrow isles to get to the cash register.

Todd had paid the bill and when they left the restaurant he placed his hand possessively on Shelby's lower back as they walked towards his car. He opened the door for her and when they were both in, Todd turned in his seat and looked at Shelby.

"Are you tired? I have to work in the morning, but if you want to, we could watch a little more TV."

Shelby hadn't wanted the night to end yet and she was so glad that Todd had made the suggestion.

"No, I'm not tired; I'm usually working later than this. Come on up and we'll see if we can find something on one of the three channels I have."

Todd knew what it was like not to be able to afford cable and they both laughed in understanding.

It only took a few minutes to get from the restaurant to Shelby's apartment building. There was a noticeable silence in the car as the tension began to build in anticipation of what lay ahead for them. They parked on the street curb. Todd got out of the car and ran around to the passenger side so that he could open the door for Shelby. Before he got there, Shelby had already started to open it as she wasn't expecting him to open the door for her. This was all new to her. After she realized what he was doing, she let go of the door handle and waited patiently while Todd finished opening it. When she looked up, smiling warmly and ready to thank him, she saw him reach out his hand towards her, offering to help her out of the car. She laid her right hand into the upturned palm of his left hand and stepped slowly out of the car while continuing to gaze into Todd's face. The nearby street light was shining and she could see him clearly. He looked so handsome, warm and kind.

Shelby murmured her thanks and in that moment, as they looked deeply into each others eyes, so much was expressed between the two of them. There was an invitation into each others hearts and soles. A welcoming, an acceptance and an agreement to take the next step into each others lives. There wasn't any question in Shelby's mind whether or not she should be permitting Todd to come up to her apartment, knowing what may happen. It felt right.

Shelby stepped back and allowed Todd to close the car door. They walked to the entryway of the apartment building and he turned the door knob and pushed the door inward so they could enter. Inside, there was a single, bare light bulb hanging from the ceiling that lit the stairway that led to several apartments.

As they started going up the stairs side by side, Todd reached for Shelby's hand. Their fingers entwined so naturally it was as if they had done so hundreds of times. The entryway was too dark for Shelby to see the expression on Todd's face very well, but she could feel the nervous smile on her own face. She could also feel her heart start to race again and she hoped that soon he would be holding her tightly in his arms, kissing her as he had done before.

After they got into the apartment and took off their boots and coats, Shelby walked over and turned the TV on. She was switching the channel and was about to ask Todd if he wanted anything to drink when suddenly she felt his hands on her hips. Shelby was pleasantly surprised to feel that possessive grip of his hands on her. He turned her around and kissed her with an intensity that was even stronger than the first time their lips met. Shelby brought her hands up and raked her fingers through his long dark hair. She could feel the soft tickle of his mustache as soon as their lips met.

Her lips parted, her mouth warm and welcoming. Their mouths melded together as their lips and tongues began greedily exploring. Todd's hands moved slowly up her waist, up further across her ribs and stopped at the softness of her breasts. His lips trailed kisses across her cheek and down her throat, to the gentle curve of her neck. He nipped her ever so slightly with his teeth and when he did, Shelby gasped. She was overwhelmed with the strong pull of desire and moaned as she dropped her head back in submission. She gently pushed him back away from her, steadied herself, then reached for his hand and led him into her bedroom.

They quickly removed their clothing and Todd pulled Shelby tightly to him as his lips took possession of hers. They fell onto the bed still entwined in each others arms. When their mouths momentarily separated to catch their breath, Todd moved his lips over to her ear as his hands began to explore each curve of her body. Although Shelby's eyes were closed, she couldn't have seen even if they had been open. Her head was dizzy, her blood was pumping and she was breathing heavily. She had never felt this kind of desire.

Afterwards, their passion spent, Todd nestled his face into the crook of her neck between her long sensuous neck and her soft shoulder. His lips pressed against her throat as he laid down on her, fighting to catch his breath. They were both covered in a fine sheen of sweat, and could feel each others hearts racing as they panted for air. Gloriously exhausted, the lovers fell to sleep wrapped in each other's arms, knowing they were meant to be together.

* * *

Chapter Five

Todd woke early the next morning. He felt Shelby's warm body next to him. His chest was pressed to her back, his arm encircled her waist and his hand lay gently beneath her breast. Shelby's hair spread over the pillowcase and Todd couldn't contain the need to nuzzle his face into her hair and breathe in its sweet raspberry scent.

Shelby woke slowly. She couldn't remember ever sleeping so soundly and feeling so resplendent. She felt Todd's nearness and she brought her hand up, laid it along his hip and drew him closer to her. Wanting to be held in his arms, Shelby turned towards him and laid her face gently on his chest. In unison, their arms and legs entwined around each other and their hands tenderly caressed each others back. Shelby was immersed in the moment and could have stayed just as they were forever, but as if realizing all good things must come to an end, Todd lifted his head to look at the alarm clock on the stand near Shelby's bed. Then he dropped his head back onto the pillow and moaned.

"I hate to say this, but I have to get moving. I have to be to work soon."

"Do you have to go? It can't be that busy at the campground."

"Normally it wouldn't be, but there are a lot of hunters there this weekend, the cabins are booked full." Todd lifted his head and looked into Shelby's eyes. "I'll be back after work okay?"

Shelby looked back into his eyes and smiled. "You'd better. I'll even go to the store and we'll have some dinner when you get here."

"I'd be happy to just have you, but dinner sounds great." He kissed her deeply and although he knew he was running short on time, it was hard for him to pull away from her warmth. Finally, he groaned and rolled off the bed. "I have to leave or I'm going to be late. I'll see you later."

Shelby lay on her side with the sheet held loosely in her fist which was nestled on her chest. She watched Todd walk to the pile of clothes that lay on the floor where they had been hastily discarded the previous evening. His muscles were lean and tight from his broad shoulders down to his narrow hips. She felt the strong tug of desire build in her just looking at him. As he dressed, she smiled lazily and said. "Yeah, later."

After he dressed, Todd bent over and gave her one last kiss then, reluctantly left.

Shelby knew she had a lot to do if she was going to get to the store and figure out a meal to put together before that afternoon, but she couldn't help basking in the warmth and splendor of her bed. She sinuously stretched the entire length of her body like a svelte cat, waking from its nap. She felt so wonderfully sated. She began thinking about the glorious night she had just spent with Todd. She reveled in the memory of his lips and fingers exploring her body, leaving her breathless and yearning for their bodies to join once more. That was how she had always imagined it would be like when a man truly made love to you.

Finally, she slowly pulled herself from her bed and felt like she was gliding as she walked to the front door to lock it. She then went into her bathroom and got into her shower. Her body felt relaxed yet exhilarated and when she brought her hands up and placed them on her cheeks, she could feel their warmth and instinctively knew she was beaming with a rosy glow.

Every day after that, Shelby and Todd fell into an easy routine of spending every available minute they had with each other. Those moments weren't filled with the frenzy of going places and doing things. Instead, they settled into a quiet existence, together, in her apartment, making love. Occasionally, they would tear themselves away from each other and go out and have a few drinks or go dancing with some friends of Todd's. But, on each occasion, when he drank, he seemed to run into one type of conflict or another. It made Shelby very uncomfortable.

Once, in the middle of a perfectly wonderful night while they were out at a dance club, Todd decided to put himself between a woman and her boyfriend, in the pretence of defending her honor. In all actuality, the boyfriend was just drunk and acting foolish and when Todd started pushing the boyfriend backward, Todd's friends had to quickly pull him away before a fight ensued. The couple were quite confused and taken aback by what Todd had done. Due to what happened, the establishment asked him to leave.

Another time, they had gone shopping at the mall and Shelby, noticing the billboard of the movie theatre that was also in the mall, asked Todd if they could watch one of the movies playing. He agreed, but since the movie didn't start for almost two more hours, they decided to go have dinner at the café style steakhouse that was in the middle of the mall. They had tender and delicious beef tips to eat plus a small piece of cheesecake for dessert. Afterwards, they still had a little time to spare before the movie started, so Todd suggested they go to the bar area and have a beer which they served in a frosted glass. While Shelby sipped slowly at her drink, Todd was finishing his third beer and was almost ready to order a fourth when Shelby reminded him that the movie would be starting. Todd reluctantly paid the bar tab and they walked to the theatre.

They bought their tickets and went in to find seats. Although Shelby was eager to see the movie, Todd seemed to have had a change of heart and fifteen minutes into the show, he grabbed her arm and said. "Come on, I'm leaving, this movie is stupid."

To avoid making a scene and bothering other patrons, Shelby gave a slight nod to her head and followed Todd's lead out the exit door.

She wanted to ask him what that was about. Why he had just got up and left when they'd only been there long enough to see the previews of upcoming movies and a few minutes of the show. But, she was so disheartened; she simply got into the car and sat in silence during their drive back to the apartment. Todd drove recklessly on the way home and seemed as unconcerned about that as he was about disappointing Shelby and ruining her evening. He had just finished asking her if she wanted to stop down to the bowling alley for one last drink before they went back to the apartment when suddenly, red flashing lights and the alerting sirens of a police car came up quickly behind them.

Shelby looked at Todd nervously, realizing how much the next few minutes would affect his chance to become an officer of the law.

Fortunately, Todd humbled himself and treated the police chief with respect. He was lucky, he could have easily been arrested for driving while impaired but it appeared to Shelby that something knowing passed between them, like an unstated warning. Todd was given a speeding ticket and was visibly shaken as the officer drove away in his patrol car. Thus ended another infrequent excursion out of the apartment for an evening out.

The next day, Todd was back to the man Shelby loved. As usual, he didn't apologize, but he did act as if he understood he came close to really messing things up, both with Shelby and his future career. He seemed to turn on every ounce of charm he had and Shelby was blown away by how sweet and loving he was. He attempted to make her a breakfast of eggs and toast, which were both a little burned, but Shelby decided it was the thought that counted. Afterwards, they snuggled on the couch until mid afternoon when they both had to get ready to go to work.

These few experiences taught Shelby that going out on a date wasn't everything it was cracked up to be. Love and relationships just seemed to be easier when you didn't have to deal with distractions and negative influences. At least theirs was. Because of this understanding, Shelby didn't mind the quiet nights alone with Todd.

By the time Christmas came, Shelby and Todd felt their relationship had progressed to the point where it was time for them to introduce each other to their family. They spent Christmas Eve with Shelby's parents and Todd was introduced to her family. By this time, the tension between Shelby and her parents had relaxed considerably. The separation from each other had given them the space they all needed to help their relationship mend. Therefore, they had a delicious dinner and an enjoyable evening.

Christmas morning was spent with Todd's family. Shelby quickly noticed that he seemed to be as crazy about his niece and nephew as Shelby was of hers. She thought that it was great that he was so relaxed around children and enjoyed playing with them. They had a wonderful breakfast of eggs, sausage, bacon, pancakes, toast and homemade muffins. Although Shelby was quite nervous and quiet, Todd's family went out of their way to make her feel welcome.

Along with the dynamics of his and her families, came Shelby's introduction to Mark's family. There wasn't any hesitation about agreeing to go when Todd mentioned that they had been invited to Christmas dinner. Shelby knew he had considered them his second family and that he would have been disappointed if they didn't go. At the same time, Shelby was admittedly filled with trepidation about meeting Mark's sister, whom Todd has professed to want to marry. As much as she wanted to pretend it didn't matter, it did. She wished he had never mentioned anything because if Shelby hadn't known, she wouldn't have the burden of pretending she didn't know.

Throughout the time spent at Mark's mothers, Shelby felt welcome and the dinner itself was delicious. There wasn't even the slightest hint of underlying hostility or scrutiny so Shelby just sat back and listened to the bantering of the large family and enjoyed the evening.

With the Christmas holiday over with, along with the initial family introductions, Shelby sat on her couch thinking how this had been the happiest Christmas she could remember having. Sharing the holidays with someone you love just seemed to make all the difference in the world. She couldn't stop smiling.

In the solitude of their days together, Shelby and Todd held hands as they talked and got to know each other. They shared their pasts, mostly the disappointments and disillusionments. They shared their fears and their weaknesses and their hopes for the future. The more they grew to know each other, the more they trusted each other with their vulnerabilities. They wanted to help each other heal from the emotional wounds they had suffered.

Although Shelby wasn't completely sure what she could possibly do to be of help to Todd, she knew for sure that she was completely in love with him and would do whatever was in her power to prove to him that he was worthy of unconditional love. Shelby could sense that like her, Todd's confidence in himself had been shattered by events and relationships in his past. She could also sense his goodness and planned on treating him with all the respect and kindness that he deserved. Hopefully, in doing so, he would start believing that he deserved it too.

With Todd, Shelby felt wanted and needed. The love she gave was finally being returned. This is what she had longed for as long as she could remember. It was as if they were destined for each other. God had brought them together to mend their hearts and to bring true joy and happiness into their lives.

Shelby was still deep in thought when the phone rang. She jumped up to answer it figuring it was Todd calling from work.

"Hey, stranger. Where've you been? No one's seen you much since you started dating Todd." Diane was snickering as she asked.

"Oh Diane, I know, I never thought I'd ever meet a guy like Todd."

"Sounds like you've really fallen for him. Do you think you'll still be heading to Florida next week?"

Shelby's face dropped, the smile was gone and the reverie of her time with Todd quickly evaporated like the sudden explosion of a bubble bursting.

"Oh my God, I forgot. Oh Diane. What am I going to do?"

"Well, we made plans to leave this town because there was nothing that kept us here. I guess you'd better think about it and figure out if that's still true for you or not." Diane said compassionately.

After Shelby hung up the phone, she sat on the couch and drew her knees up to her chest. She laid her head on her knees and kept asking herself over and over, what am I going to do?

Even though Todd had turned her life in a completely different direction than it was going a month earlier, Shelby couldn't deny that the decision she had made to move to Florida had made so much sense. It felt like the right thing to do and she was confident that she had made the right decision. Now, she was so torn. Her heart couldn't bear the thought of being separated from Todd; yet, she had made plans with Diane and didn't want to disappoint her either. Her relationship with Todd was everything she had dreamt of. She had never felt so happy and complete. Could she allow all of this to slip through her fingers?

That evening Todd met her at the bowling alley just as she was finishing for the night. He noticed that she seemed unusually quiet and his protective feelings for her instinctively kicked in. He began to feel defensive, wondering if someone had bothered her that evening at work and upset her.

As soon as Shelby saw that Todd was there to pick her up, she stuck her head into the bar doorway to tell the bartender that she was leaving. They left through the exit door of the lanes area again as she really wanted to get out of there and didn't want to take a chance that either she or Todd would get caught up in a conversation with the regulars in the bar.

As soon as they got outside, Todd took a gentle grip on Shelby's elbow and pulled her into his arms. "Are you alright Shelb? You seem upset."

"Oh Todd," Shelby said in a distressing tone as she fought back tears. "Diane called this morning." At Todd's questioning and worrisome look, she went on. "She reminded me that we had planned on heading to Florida right after New Year's Day - that's next week!"

Todd held Shelby tightly in his arms, his heart pounding with emotion as he tried to gather his thoughts. In a matter of minutes, he had gone from thinking someone had upset Shelby, to the unsettling reminder that she might soon be leaving. He felt unsteady, as though his legs were about to give way. He thanked God that he was holding on to Shelby, that she was in his arms. It seemed to steady him.

"Come on," he said as he turned her. Keeping his arm around her waist, he held her tightly as he led her through the crunchy snow to the passenger door of his car. He had never seen her upset like this. Although she was a quiet person, she normally seemed so strong and confident. It worried him to see her so confused and bewildered. "Let's go to my place and we'll figure it out," he said in what he hoped was his most reassuring tone of voice. "Is that okay with you?"

Shelby nodded her head. Todd gave her a little kiss on the forehead and opened the car door. Shelby climbed in and slid down into the icy seat. She was shivering and as she put her gloved hands deeply into her coat pockets, she leaned back onto the headrest and stared blankly out of the side window.

As their minds were lost in thought, the ride to Todd's was stilled in silence except for the hard rock music playing on the radio. Once they got inside his place and took off their coats and boots he asked her if she wanted him to turn on the cassette player with some music he had taped. Suddenly, all Shelby could think about were the women he might have played those songs for before and the ones that he'd be playing them for after she left. She didn't tell him this. She only shook her head no. He grasped her hand and pulled her over to the couch where they sat with his arm protectively around her. He cupped her chin with his other hand and brought it up so that they were looking in each other's eyes.

"I guess if you still want to go, I'll understand. But," he said, his voice deepening. "If you change your mind when you get there, just let me know, I'll fly you back, okay?"

Never had Shelby heard or imagined she would ever hear words that sounded as sweet and loving as those that Todd had just spoken. Neither could she imagine that she could feel as loved as she felt at that moment. Yes, she was very much in love with Todd and she could read it in his eyes, he loved her too. There was no doubt about what she was going to do, she was being held in the arms of the man she loved, she didn't need or want to leave, this is where she wanted to be.

After a passionate night together, Todd took Shelby back to her apartment in the morning before he went to work. They kissed warmly and said their good-byes. As soon as she was in the living room, she went to the phone and called Diane.

"Hey, it's me," she said apologetically, the feeling of guilt heavy in her voice. "I'm so sorry, Diane I don't mean to mess up our plans, but I'm not going to Florida. I'm staying here." She braced herself for Diane's reply. Would she be angry with her? Would she lose a good friend over her change of plans?

"I knew you were going to say that," Diane said in an oddly breathless tone.

Shelby cringed, gripping the telephone receiver tightly, but before she could explain, Diane continued.

"But you know? It's okay." Unexpectedly, Diane laughed in delight. "We might both regret it someday," she managed to get out through her laughter. "But I just got a good job offer and I've decided to stay too."

Shelby smiled and sighed with relief.

* * *

Chapter Six

Shelby and Todd spent New Year's Eve together at a party held at the home of a friend of his family. Shelby wore the long white evening gown she had worn at her graduation. She felt lovely. She had wanted to make a good impression with his family and friends. She was initially nervous about the party but, one look from Todd's approving eyes as he arrived at the apartment to pick her up, set her mind at ease. At the party, Todd was never far away from her. He held her hand or stood next to her with his hand possessively around her waist. Their warm glances and smiles towards each other throughout the evening left no doubt in anyone's mind that they were very much in love.

Although Shelby had never been very outgoing and chatty, she felt surprisingly comfortable with all of these people. It was amazing how many of them had ties to her own family from long ago. With the help of a couple drinks to set her more at ease, and the confidence she felt with Todd by her side, the evening couldn't have gone more smoothly.

Now that the bustle of the holidays had passed, Shelby knew that she had to figure out where she was going to live. Since she had planned all along on moving to Florida, she had told the landlord that she wouldn't need the apartment after the first of January. A few weeks ago, he'd casually mentioned that he had a new renter ready to move in; so she knew she couldn't extend her lease. Moving back in with her parents just didn't seem like a viable option. She had been so excited and ready to move out on her own that she couldn't see herself moving back again.

When Todd arrived that night after work, the worries of where she would go left her mind as he climbed into bed and pulled her into his arms. She was soon to find out that Todd had been thinking about the same problem.

As Shelby lay with her head on Todd's chest and his arms wrapped around her, he said softly, but with the hint of excitement. "I stopped by to see my sister before I came here tonight."

"Yeah?" Shelby murmured lazily, enjoying the feeling of being in Todd's arms. "Did you just stop by to say hi or is something the matter with Darcy?"

"Everything's fine," he reassured her. "I just had an idea and I wanted to see what she thought about it."

Shelby's curiosity started to peak, but she didn't know whether she had the right to pry and ask him what their discussion was about. So, she just nodded her head slightly as if in acknowledgment that she was listening to him talk.

"I had mentioned to Kyle the other day that you had to move out of your apartment, just to get a feel for how he might react if I asked if you could move in with me. But, before I got a chance to ask him, he must have had an idea what I was going to ask. He immediately jumped in and told me that he hoped you found a place okay, but that he wouldn't want any chick in his apartment. Then, he said that maybe this was a chance for me to find a place to move, with you."

Shelby's eyes shot open and her heart began to race with excitement, but she didn't move a muscle as she listened intently and let him continue.

"Then I remembered that Darcy has a spare bedroom at her house. I stopped by tonight and told her that you needed to be out of your place in a few days and asked her if it would be alright if you and I moved into her spare bedroom until we found another place to live."

Shelby finally raised her head and looked at Todd with nervous and questioning eyes. Although they spent most of their time together, the thought of actually moving in together was a pretty huge step in their relationship. She had no idea that Todd was as ready to take this next step as she was. She found herself giddy with happiness. Todd cared enough about her to find a place for her to move to and, he wanted to move in with her too. Shelby's heart was beating fast and she felt breathless. She forced herself to calm down since she wasn't sure what his sister's answer had been. Shelby decided she better get a grip on herself and find out all the facts before leaping into his arms. What if Darcy had said no?

Todd was trying to read Shelby's lack of reaction. She wasn't saying anything; she was just staring at him with expressionless eyes. It was starting to make him nervous. Maybe he'd read her wrong and she didn't want to move in with him. Hopefully she just didn't understand what he was suggesting. "Darcy said she didn't mind if we moved in for a while." Todd said, uncertainty making him speak slowly. "What do you think?"

Todd watched as Shelby's eyes lit up as if she had been given an elegantly wrapped gift. Color flushed her cheeks and her mouth curved upwards in delight. She suddenly threw herself on him. Catching him off guard, the force rolled Todd flat onto his back. He welcomed her delight and held her tightly when her arms wrapped around his neck.

"Oh Todd," she said with glee. "Thank you."

Todd held Shelby tightly; he could feel the dampness of her happy tears as she buried her face against his neck. "So, I take it you think it's a good idea?" he teased her.

"Yes," she sniffed.

Her face was still hidden, but Todd felt the smile against his flesh.

"I'd love to move in with you."

He held her for a few minutes while she regained control.

Shelby released her strangle hold from around Todd's neck and then looked lovingly into his eyes. "I'm just so overwhelmed," she finally managed to admit. "Moving in with you… and your sister." Shelby said, wonder in her voice. "She's helping us…me."

Todd pulled Shelby against him. His nervousness disappeared and he smiled at the thought of them being together. He kissed her deeply, showing all the love and passion he felt. There weren't any thoughts in his mind or heart about how quickly their relationship was moving, only that they were going to be together.

Shelby woke the next morning in the warmth of Todd's arms. She laid there dreamily thinking that even though she had to go to work later that evening; Todd had the day off so they would be able to spend a luxurious day together. By mid-morning, they were both finally feeling the effects of not eating any dinner the evening before, so they reluctantly got out of bed and went to the kitchen to get something to eat. Throughout the morning, Shelby noticed that Todd was more quiet than usual. In the back of her mind she wondered whether he was starting to realize the big step they were about to be making by moving in together and was second guessing his decision. She shook off the thought, what was she thinking? She hadn't asked him to find her a new place to move in to. She hadn't even thought about moving in with him, much less said anything to make him think that's what they should do. So, why would he be questioning his own idea? She realized that she was probably just reading something into his quietness that wasn't there. Never did she expect to hear what he said as he was getting dressed.

"I have to leave for a while. Are you going to hang around here and finish packing today?"

Shelby was a little stunned. Although they hadn't talked about it any more that morning, she thought they would probably be going over to his sisters to take a few of the boxes that she had already packed. The suddenness of the way Todd mentioned that he had something planned, as well as the fact that he was doing everything he could not to look at her when he made the statement, made her have the same anxious feeling as she did earlier in the morning. A sort of dread hit her in the gut. Was she just imagining all this? Or was something going on?

Todd sat on the couch to put his socks and boots on. "I have to drive up to Allentown today." He hesitated while tying the laces on his boots, then continued as he slipped his arms into the sleeves of his coat. His words came out quickly, his voice quiet and shaky. "I've been dating a girl since high school. She's going to the university there, and I have to tell her in person that it's over between us."

Shelby felt like she'd just been punched. Was he saying that he had another girlfriend the entire time they had been together? Had everything he'd been saying all this time been a lie? Shelby all but fell on the couch, hitting the old cushions hard and quick, like she had been shoved back by the impact of his words. She looked at him, her eyes filled with confusion and shock. She gulped and her voice was shaky when she said. "Todd, what are you talking about?"

He finally looked at her, although he wished he hadn't. There was a visible look of pain on her face that seemed to be pleading for an answer. As he didn't know how to explain his own actions, let alone answer her question, he nonchalantly shrugged his shoulders and smiled. His voice was light and calm when he said. "Look, it's no big deal, I haven't been out with her since I met you, but I have to go see her and tell her it's over in person."

He walked over to Shelby and pulled her hands gently to help her stand. He pulled her into his arms and held her warmly, like nothing unusual had been said or done. "I'll see you later." He gave her a quick kiss and then, just like that, he left.

Shelby once again collapsed onto the couch. She couldn't believe Todd had thrown all of this at her then left before she even had time to process what he'd just told her. She had so many confusing thoughts and feelings going through her mind that she felt dizzy. Todd had just left, to spend the afternoon with a girlfriend. A girlfriend that she didn't even know existed. She started to fill with doubt and despair. How could this be happening? Who was this girl? Had he really not seen her since they'd met? Did he and this girlfriend talk on the phone? Why hadn't he broken up with her before? Why did he have to go explain all this in person? Did he expect me to just say okay and not worry about it?

Shelby paced through the apartment for hours; the questions continuing to rush in her head. Why wasn't he back yet? Where was he? What is going on? Is he making up with her?

All of Shelby's newfound feelings of completeness and her renewed self confidence fell by the wayside. All she could think was, my God, why had she allowed herself to fall in love again. Hadn't she learned by now that every time she thought a guy really cared for her, she'd been hurt and humiliated? Hadn't she finally convinced herself to change and not be used again? Had she fallen back into the same hole to crawl out of again? Hadn't she finally realized that having a loving relationship just wasn't in the cards for her?

Although Shelby watched the hands on the clock slowly tick away the minutes, she was so preoccupied that she didn't realize how late in the afternoon it was getting. She suddenly realized that she had to be to work in a half hour. As upset as she was, she knew that she couldn't call in sick this late, so she quickly changed her shirt, pulled her hair up into a ponytail, pulled on her coat and boots and walked to work. She drudged through the snow, slowly putting one foot in front of the other. Her head was bent low as she stared at the ground in front of her. She couldn't even feel the coldness of the winter wind whipping at her. She had a hard time shaking off the dark mood she was in, but she knew she had to before she started working.

Even though she had been distracted throughout the night, Shelby was actually thankful that she had gone to work. If she had stayed home, she would have just ended up pacing the floors of her apartment, worrying all evening. At least working allowed her to occupy her thoughts with something else for a few hours.

As her work shift was ending, Shelby saw Todd coming through the doors in the bar area. She didn't know what to do, all of the anxiety that she had felt earlier that day came back full force, making her upset and scared. She didn't know whether to be angry at him for being so insensitive to how she felt or whether to be afraid that she may lose him to this other woman. If that was the case, she knew she would have to numb her heart and mind so that she could deal with it. That was the way she had always had to deal with rejection before. Whatever the case, she just couldn't allow herself to dwell on it any more. She had almost made herself physically sick thinking about it all day and she knew she couldn't worry like that any more. Shelby tried to ignore Todd's presence. She turned away from him and bent over the table to finish wiping it off.

As he approached her, he cheerfully said. "Hi."

Shelby pushed the chair under the table and then turned around to face him. She stood there motionless with the dishrag in her hand, looking at him as he continued to walk towards her.

When he reached her, he smiled and acted as if nothing was wrong.

Shelby searched his face to see what she could read from it. His eyes had the same warmth in them she had seen the night before, and the smirk-like, crooked smile of his was there just as it had been before. He reached for her hand, and as he gripped it tightly, her heart skipped a beat.

She wanted to pull her hand back, but it betrayed her. She loved when her hand was wrapped tightly in his. The strength of his fingers and the power of his hands, felt like a warm, soothing and protective shield. Shelby's fingers automatically twined through his.

She couldn't force a smile onto her lips and it was very hard for her to control her feelings. Her voice was flat and void of emotion as she said. "I didn't know if I'd see you tonight or not."

The smile quickly fell from Todd's face and was replaced with concern and nervousness. He gripped her hand tighter as he said softly. "I told you I'd see you later didn't I?"

Shelby looked down at the ground as she felt the façade of her strength begin to crumble. Her voice was shaky as she replied. "Yeah, but…"

Todd quickly jumped in; as if he had a strong feeling he knew what she was worried about. "Everything is taken care of Shelb. Come on, you ready to go home?"

Shelby's lips quivered and she knew that the tears she had held back all day were about to fall. She didn't want him to know how scared she had been that he might not be back. She also didn't want him to know how she had been anguishing all day about what he was saying and doing with this other woman. She wrapped her arms around his neck and hid her face in his neck. The strength of his arms around her, the feel of his body close to her, and the warmth of his breath against her neck dried her tears and filled the emptiness in her heart again.

When they got to the apartment, they fell into each other's arms and kissed with all the passion and need of two lovers that had been separated by circumstance and rejoined by fate. After their ardor had been spent and they lay in each other's arms, Shelby silently wished she had the courage to question him. There were answers she needed about this other woman and the long day he had spent with her. But as she lay with her body facing Todd's, with their legs entwined and his arms wrapped gently around her, she wondered how she could question the depth of his feelings and love for her. Besides, he didn't give her the impression that he was going to talk about the situation. He acted as if there was no reason for her to get upset or concerned. She started to think that maybe it was just her lack of confidence in herself that kept these feeling of unrest churning inside her. Clearing the thoughts and questions from her mind, Shelby fell into a deep sleep. The emotional peaks and valleys of that day had exhausted her and she desperately needed a long dreamless night of rest.

* * *

Chapter Seven

The move was complete, not that there had been all that much to do. Most of the furniture Shelby had, came with the apartment. So she only had her TV, along with her personal items to move. She couldn't say she was all that comfortable moving in with Todd's sister and her family, but she realized she didn't have many options open to her since she'd waited so long to change her mind about moving to Florida.

Shelby got everything settled comfortably in their new bedroom, and she and Todd even bought the latest craze, a shag comforter for their bed. It was warm, but very impractical as they woke up every morning with strands of the long fabric on their mouths. It always brought a smile to Shelby's face to wake up to the sight of Todd with a blue fuzzy mouth. He slept heavily and never even stirred when Shelby gently wiped the thread from his lips. Then she would inevitably feel compelled to kiss those same lips softly and gaze lovingly at him. She was always so tempted to run her fingers through his thick dark hair and push its tumbled strands away from his handsome face. But, he looked so peaceful; she didn't want to chance disturbing his deep sleep. Instead, she nuzzled up next to him to enjoy these first moments of each day before she rose.

The month passed by quickly. Although Shelby felt more comfortable with Darcy and her family, both she and Todd agreed that it was time to find another place to live. Upon arriving home after a long night of work, and retiring to their little corner of the world, Shelby lay contently in Todd's arms. The love she felt for him never diminished, she felt secure and safe in his strong arms. Normally, they fell asleep after making love, but tonight Todd talked excitedly about his plans to apply to a local police department. His voice was very animated and Shelby knew that if the lights had been on, she would have seen the sparkle and determination in his eyes. He was obviously very psyched about the prospect of becoming a police officer. Shelby got caught up in his enthusiasm and encouraged him by telling him how proud she was of him, and how confident she was that he'd not only get the job, but be a fine officer. She pledged her support as they were aware that his work schedule would be very erratic and that most likely, he would get stuck on the graveyard shift.

Todd kissed Shelby's forehead, then rolled towards the edge of the bed so he could reach up and turn on the light that was on the nightstand. He was wide awake now. Shelby's support and encouragement made him believe that it wasn't just a far fetched dream, that it actually would be possible for his dream to become a reality. Todd turned back so he was lying on his side, facing Shelby with his head propped on his bent left arm. His face was close to hers and he looked lovingly into her eyes. There was a hint of nervousness in his voice as he realized that his destiny, the path he was supposed to be following had become very clear to him.

"I know most of my friends can't believe I want to be a cop, but it's something I really want to do." As he continued, he brought his hand up, ran his fingers through Shelby's long hair and then tucked it behind her ear. "You know, a lot of things seem to be coming together lately." He dipped his head and whispered. "I met you, and now I know what career I want to have. My life seems to have a direction now. Oh Shelby, I really love you."

Tears filled Shelby's eyes and threatened to overflow. She was chocked up at the thought that she had made a difference in someone's life. Suddenly her life also seemed to have a purpose. She raised her hand and laid it gently on Todd's cheek. "I love you so much Todd. I've never been so happy in my life."

He kissed her lips softly. His eyes were glistening with emotion. "Me neither. I didn't plan on saying this Shelb, but it seems like the right time. Will you marry me?" He kissed her on the temple after the words spilled from his lips and then pulled her into his arms and held her tightly.

Shelby's eyes closed and her tears of happiness slid slowly down her face. A smile came to her lips and her heart skipped a beat. She felt a warmth and love that surpassed anything she had ever experienced before. Instead of being shocked or surprised, she felt a warm sense of fulfillment. As if the emptiness in her life was gone and that the part of her life that was missing, was now found. She felt complete; it was as if this was the next natural step for them to take. There was no doubt about the happiness that filled her. She turned her face towards Todd, wrapped her arms around his neck and kissed him tenderly.

"Yes, I'll marry you."

Shelby woke the following morning to the feel of Todd's hands on her – tickling her. She squirmed and wiggled, hysterical with laughter under his relentless fingers.

"Come on and get up, we're going uptown to get a ring." he said when he finally stopped.

Shelby looked up at him with wide, gleefully happy eyes. "You mean it?"

Todd ran his fingers through his hair, pushing it away from his forehead so that his dark, sparkling eyes could be seen. He smiled mischievously at her. "Of course I mean it. Come on."

He jumped out of bed, grabbing Shelby's hand and pulling her along with him. They inched the bedroom door open and listened for any sign that Darcy and her family were there, but all was quiet. They had already left for daycare and work. So, Todd and Shelby laughed as they ran down the hallway and into the bathroom so they could hop into the shower together.

They drove to a small jewelry shop on the main street in Smithville. There were diamond rings of all sizes and prices but the jeweler instinctively motioned them towards the case with the less expensive rings in it. His experience must have told him that they were not only young, but 'living on love' rather than the riches of a couple who were financially stable. They picked out a ring with a diamond that was barely big enough to flicker in the bright overhead lights but to Shelby, it was the most beautiful ring she had ever seen. She smiled at Todd with the happiness only a girl who is newly engaged can feel.

Todd put the ring in its small velvet lined box and put it in his coat pocket as they left the shop. When they got back in the car, Todd looked at Shelby. His eyes again sparkled with mischievous as he smiled at her. He pulled the box out of his pocket and passed it back and forth, from hand to hand.

"I should probably wait ten more days to give you this so we can be officially engaged on Valentine's Day don't you think?"

Shelby looked at him with questioning and pleading eyes. "Oh Todd, you aren't really going to make me wait that long to wear my ring are you?"

Not being able to contain the exuberance he was feeling about getting married to Shelby he said. "No, I'm just kidding, I want you to wear it right now."

So Todd took the ring out of the box and gently guided it onto Shelby's finger. Shelby thought Todd looked like his chest was about to burst with pride. The crooked smile, hidden behind his mustache, along with the gleam in his eyes, told her that he truly wanted to take this next step as much as she did.

On the ride home, Shelby leaned back on her headrest and looked dreamily out the side window. The smile on her face and the fullness in her heart, expressed the happiness that she was feeling. She had never felt like this before and she was relishing the sensation of their deep love. Here they were, only a couple months into their relationship and already they were engaged and ready to walk down the isle. Even in her wildest dreams, she couldn't have imagined anything this perfect happening.

Unfortunately, when they told everyone their good news, not many of their friends or their families, shared their exuberance. Shelby and Todd went to her parents first. They sat down at the kitchen table and as Louise was pouring coffee into each of their cups, she said. "So, what are you two up to today? Did you come to town to get some groceries?"

"No." Shelby hesitated until her mother had set the carafe of coffee back on the counter. "We stopped by to tell you that we just got engaged. Isn't it wonderful? We're going to get married!"

Shelby's parents looked at each other questioningly and then back at Shelby and Todd. Louise's eyebrows were raised in an expression of shock and her dad's eyebrows were scrunched together to form a deep V on his forehead as if in anger or at least deeply contemplating what he had just been told.

"Well?" Shelby said. She was expecting congratulations and hugs.

"Well, that's just wonderful." Louise hesitantly said as she tried to force a smile to her lips.

"Uh hum," Shelby's dad cleared his throat and then slowly said with concern in his voice. "Yes, we know how happy you've been Shelby, and we really do like you Todd. But, don't you think this is a little soon to be getting married? You've only known each other a couple months."

"I know," Todd said wistfully, not reading the hesitancy in her father's voice. "It amazes me how much I love Shelby. I want to spend the rest of my life with her."

"Well," Shelby's dad said as his eyebrows returned to their normal position. "When you put it like that, what can I say but congratulations?" And with that, he brought his hand forward to shake Todd's then they all stood up and hugged each other.

When they stopped in at Todd's mother's to share their good news, they were again met with an initial look of shock. There was a moment of hesitation before his mother stuttered. "Well, I don't know you too well Shelby, but it really doesn't matter whether I like you or not. As long as Todd loves you and you love him, that's all that matters." She gave them a weak smile, and then they all stood up and embraced.

After they left, Shelby looked at Todd nervously. "She wasn't very happy was she?"

Todd smiled, wrapped his arm around Shelby's shoulder, drew her close and then laughed. "Don't worry about it. We just caught her off guard and she just didn't know what to say. She does like you."

The ease which Todd had let the comment his mother made roll off his back made Shelby feel she didn't have anything to worry about. Todd was right. The news just surprised her and she was probably so flabbergasted to hear her son say he was getting married that she didn't know what to say.

She relaxed and smiled as Todd dropped his hand from her shoulder to her hand and pulled her as he started running towards the car. When they reached it, Todd pulled Shelby into his arms. After a long embrace, he pulled back from her, lowered his face and kissed her deeply. When they finally unwound their arms, they held hands, looked deeply into each other's eyes and smiled brightly. Their eyes sparkled and the happiness they felt radiated from them.

That evening, on the way to work, Shelby stopped by Diane's house to tell her that Todd had proposed to her.

"Oh my God." Diane said as she rushed excitedly towards Shelby and pulled her into her arms to congratulate her. Then she laughed as she continued. "He moves pretty fast doesn't he? He swept you off your feet and now he wants to carry you into the sunset."

Shelby exhaled as she smiled, then said laughingly, "I guess that about sums it up. You know Diane; I never thought anything this wonderful would ever happen to me. I've never even had a steady boyfriend before I met Todd." She reached out and held Diane's hands as her expression and voice became serious and full of emotion. "I love him so much, and I'm so happy that I finally found a guy that loves me as much as I love him."

"Boy, you sure are floating on a cloud." Diane smiled warmly at her friend. "Who would have thought you'd meet and fall in love with the man of your dreams just as you were ready to give up and move away from here?"

Shelby waved good-bye to Diane as she left and continued on to work. When she arrived at the bowling alley, Shelby had to laugh at herself. She was the quintessential bride-to-be, showing off her engagement ring to almost every one of the patrons. She was indeed floating on a cloud.

After Todd arrived at work that same evening, he called Mark to tell his best friend that he had asked Shelby to marry him.

"Are you crazy or what?" Mark exclaimed with surprise.

"What do you mean?" Todd chuckled. "I'm not crazy, but I'm crazy about her. She's hot."

"Yeah," Mark said sarcastically. "Well you were crazy about Wendy too and you swore you were going to marry her. In fact, weren't you two engaged when you met Shelby?"

"That was different," Todd said, trying to dismiss Mark's point. "We had been going together for so long we just assumed we were going to get married. But, then she decided she'd rather go to college than get married right away and I didn't want to wait that long."

"No wonder she was so pissed off when you broke up with her. You said she called Shelby on the phone and gave her some shit didn't she?"

"Yeah, but I told Shelby it must have just been a crank call, that Wendy wouldn't do something like that because we hadn't seen each other in a while. Anyway, that's all done and over with. Aren't you going to congratulate me?"

"Yeah sure," Mark laughed. "I still think you're crazy, but she's a nice girl and maybe you've finally found someone who will do your cooking and cleaning like you've been looking for. Take it easy man."

As soon as Todd hung up the phone, he got another call. It was Chris who had just heard the news.

"Hey, I was just going to call you," Todd said as he leaned back in the office chair, looked upwards and laughed. "Who'd you hear it from, Mom?"

"Yeah, she called a little while ago. I think she's worried that you rushed into this engagement too quickly," Chris said in a concerned voice.

Todd really wasn't too concerned about how his mom felt, he knew she'd come around, and he didn't want Chris to worry about it. "I know, she didn't sound too happy when we told her, but I think she's just surprised. She'll get used to the idea."

"She was surprised alright, and so am I," Chris laughed then continued. "Shelby seems like a nice girl though."

"She's great and I think she's really good for me. I feel like my life has turned around since I met her."

"I can't say I haven't noticed the change in you, because I have," Chris said proudly and then the concern returned in his voice again. "I guess I just wanted to find out whether you really love her or whether you just wanted to get married so you'd have the family life you missed while you were growing up." Then, changing to a more lighthearted tone, he chuckled. "You know, you don't have to get married right away. Why don't you two just live together for a while and see where things go."

Todd took a deep breath as he took in what Chris had just reminded him of. He shrugged it off, but knew he could speak honestly and openly with his uncle. "I know we could just live together," Todd said in a serious tone. "But, I really do love her, she's the one for me. I want to marry her and have kids. Mom never got married and you're the closest thing I have ever had to a father. I can't change any of that, but I can try to have a better life for me, Shelby and our kids. Is it so wrong to want that?"

"No," Chris said with respect and understanding. "I just want you to be certain of the way you feel before you jump in with both feet."

"I'm sure about this Chris," Todd said with confidence.

"Okay then," Chris said lightheartedly. "I'm happy for you, congratulations."

Shelby's parents encouraged her to move back in with them and push back wedding plans for at least a few months. They said it was to give them time to plan a nice wedding, but Shelby was certain it was in the hopes that both she and Todd would realize they were rushing too quickly into such an important and permanent decision.

Neither Shelby nor Todd was swayed from their decision though. Shelby reluctantly moved back into her childhood home while Todd looked for a place for them to move into as soon as they were married. Shelby was sleeping at her parents, but she spent every available minute with Todd that she could.

On a sultry Saturday in July, Shelby married the love of her life. Todd was so handsome in his white tuxedo, and Shelby felt like a princess in her pearl trimmed gown and veil. They had veered away from the traditional vows of 'to honor and obey' and opted for more modern vows that emphasized friendship and respect. Todd had asked Shelby not to look directly into his eyes when they were pledging their vows, but how could she not? These weren't just words; they were feelings, truths and promises. She meant every word and she wanted Todd to know and believe that she would love him forever.

When Todd slipped the wedding ring on her finger, and their vows were sealed with a kiss, Shelby was filled with joy and peace. They were now joined spiritually, they had God's blessing. Their bodies, hearts and souls were joined as one. Shelby felt complete, and her lifelong dream to love and be loved was finally realized.

They celebrated their marriage with their family and friends at an intimate reception. Several hours later, they left for their honeymoon while their guests continued to celebrate. Tucked tightly under Shelby's arm was the bag of cards containing the money they had received as wedding gifts. Shelby's parents were going to take the presents to their house after the reception where Shelby and Todd would unwrap them when they returned from their honeymoon. These gifts of money, cookware, bedding and small appliances were the only possessions the couple owned. Todd had already made an arrangement with his aunt and uncle to move into the manager's cabin at the campgrounds where he worked. Chris and Mary were the managers, but since they owned their own home and lived nearby, they didn't need to use the cabin. Therefore it was not being lived in. It actually was a cute little A-frame cabin and the fact that it was furnished with appliances and bright colored furniture, made the decision to use it as a first home an easy one.

As they drove away from the reception in their car that had been decorated with crepe paper, tin cans and old shoes, Shelby leaned over and kissed Todd on the cheek

---

and then said excitedly. "Oh Todd, everything turned out so nice, where are we going for our honeymoon?"

"I didn't really make any plans; I thought we could just find a hotel nearby and spend the night there."

"Oh," Shelby said, the disappointment evident in her voice. She sat back in her seat and couldn't help feeling dismayed that Todd hadn't put any effort into making arrangements for them to go someplace special for their honeymoon. She hadn't expected to be going to Hawaii or on a cruise or anything like that, but they lived so close to the honeymoon capital of the world, he could have at least made a reservation for them to stay overnight in a suite overlooking the falls. Oh well, she thought. She was Todd's wife now, and she would have been happy even if they had just gone straight to their cabin. So, Shelby smiled, shook off her disappointment and started untwining her long hair that had been worn in an up-do beneath her veil.

She dug through her purse, looking for her brush and then remembered she had left it on the edge of the bathroom sink at her parents' house.

"Oh no," she said disappointedly. "I forgot my hair brush at mom and dad's; can we stop at a drug store and pick up another one?"

Todd looked at Shelby in disbelief. "How could you forget your brush? I don't know where there's a drugstore around here," he muttered. "God, I'm tired and I just wanted to find a hotel, now I'll have to drive all over hell looking for someplace to buy you a damn hair brush."

"Todd, what are you getting so mad at?" Shelby said with exasperation. "Geez, never mind, I'll just run my fingers through my hair and after I change my clothes I'll go find a brush myself."

"No," Todd huffed. "I'll find a store and we'll get one now." Then in a more relaxed voice he continued. "I'm just tired and need to go to sleep."

"I know," Shelby said sympathetically. "It's been a long day." Then she smiled and poked him in the side. "Were you up all night drinking at your bachelor party?"

"Cut it out," Todd smiled and shrugged away from Shelby's poking finger. "You just stop worrying about what I did or didn't do last night."

Shelby couldn't help but laugh as she wondered whether that might be why he didn't want her to look into his eyes during the ceremony. He probably didn't want her to know how hung over he was. At least he didn't puke or pass out during the service. With a sigh of relief, she turned and looked at her handsome husband.

Todd stopped at the next grocery store they passed and ran in and bought a brush for Shelby. They drove for another half hour and finally found a hotel that had a vacancy sign lit up. The hotel itself was rather bleak and when Todd opened the door to their room, Shelby discovered that although the room was clean and tidy, it was equally plain and unadorned. She had envisioned flowers, champagne and romance on her honeymoon and wondered if she should have made these arrangements herself instead of leaving it up to Todd to take care of.

Again, Shelby realized that it just didn't matter. She was with Todd and that was the only thing that was important. She grabbed her small suitcase and took out a change of clothing urgently wanting to get out of her long gown that she had been sweltering in the entire afternoon.

"I'm going in to take a shower," Shelby said with exasperation. "Do you want to go get something to eat when I get out? I didn't eat much at the reception and I'm getting pretty hungry now."

"Yeah, I guess so," Todd replied in a flat tone. "I wish they had room service here so we didn't need to go anywhere. But, since they don't I guess we'll have to. I think I saw a pizza shop back around the corner. We could go there okay?"

"Sounds good to me," Shelby said as she turned to go into the bathroom. As she stood in front of the large mirror, taking her beautiful gown off, she couldn't help but think back on the day. Sure there had been a few hitches here and there, but overall, everything went wonderfully. In the end, none of the little glitches mattered or were even noticed and she was now Todd's wife.

While sitting, eating their pizza, Todd admitted that he was just as hungry as Shelby was. The meal seemed to give him his second wind and his mood brightened immensely. He held Shelby's hand intimately as they left the parlor, and when they arrived back in their room, Todd pulled Shelby into her arms and kissed her passionately. It made his heart leap as he realized that this beautiful girl was his bride. When their lips parted, Todd looked into Shelby's eyes that were glazed over with passion.

"I love you Shelb," he murmured softly and tenderly.

"I love you too," she whispered.

She pulled out of Todd's arms and turned to walk towards the bed. She looked back at him, lowered her eyes demurely and reached for his hand. As soon as Todd gripped it, and wound his fingers around hers, she led him towards their marriage bed.

They fell into each other's arms and when they made love that night, Shelby felt the same magic between them that she had felt the first time they had made love. She was spellbound by her love for Todd and it reaffirmed her belief that they were destined for each other.

The following day, they arrived back at their new home, the little cabin. Shelby was so excited. This was the beginning of their new life together. She had envisioned her husband carrying her across the threshold. But, in those pretentious dreams, there weren't a set of narrow steps directly in front of the door as there were here. It would have been cumbersome and downright dangerous to carry someone up these. So, Shelby shook her head to dismiss the unrealistic dream from her mind as she followed Todd through the doorway.

Shelby moved through the front living room with a dreamy look on her face. She walked over to the built in book shelves and ran her fingers across them. She thought of the pictures and knick knacks she would soon place on them. She looked around at the lime green sofa and chair where they would sit on quiet evenings. She moved to one of the many windows in that room and opened it to let the warm summer air blow in.

She turned and walked through the doorway into the dining area and kitchen. She smiled as she looked at the sunny yellow dinette set where they would drink their morning coffee and eat their meals. The kitchen included a small apartment size refrigerator, a single sink and a small four burner stove. Shelby had never seen such a small and compact stove before and it tickled her to think of herself cooking meals there. There was a small counter with lower cupboards at a right angle to the stove and refrigerator. And there were two upper cupboards on either side of the sink. Shelby hoped that there would be enough room to store her cookware, dishes and canned goods. On second thought, she decided she would have Todd hammer some nails in the wall next to the refrigerator and hang her pots and pans there. That would open up space in the cupboards to store their small kitchen appliances.

Shelby peeked into the small room under the stairs that they would use for storage and then walked into the small bathroom. There was a small sink with a medicine cabinet over it, a toilet and a corner shower stall. No bathtub Shelby noted to herself, so it looked like she would have to devise a new plan for shaving her legs.

She backed out of the bathroom and walked to the stairway. She looked up to see the open loft with the wood planked cathedral ceiling. As she walked up the stairway, she envisioned climbing these stairs nightly with Todd on their way to bed. When she arrived at the top of the stairway, Shelby looked around at the open and spacious area. There was a dresser that was the same shade of yellow as the dinette set, and the double bed that had been set up in the spare room at his sister's was there.

Shelby turned around in a circle, with her eyes closed and her arms spread out at her sides. This was her home now. Her first home with Todd. It was cheerful and the perfect size for the two lovers.

A few weeks after their wedding, Todd was hired at the city police department and worked as he hoped he would, as a police officer. He worked odd days and hours as he was also attending the basic training course for police officers at a local community college. Within a month of their wedding, Shelby found out she was pregnant with their first child. They couldn't have been more happy and excited. This is what they had both longed for, marriage and a family. With their expenses at a minimum, Shelby was able to stay home during her pregnancy. She helped him with the homework and reports he was assigned at basic training and she was the perfect little housewife. She cooked meals from recipes she obtained from the new cookbooks she had received at her bridal shower and kept the little cabin clean and tidy. Todd always emphasized the importance of keeping their home clean and having his meals prepared when he got home from school. He had agreed to let her stay at home rather than work during her pregnancy if she kept up the housekeeping duties. Shelby was enjoying her new role as wife and expectant mother and never thought anything about Todd's insistence about having a clean house. She enjoyed having a clean house just as much as he did. She wouldn't have had it any other way.

The months rolled by quickly. Todd wasn't able to spend many hours at home, between the off-hour shifts of a police officer and his classes at the academy. He frequently was only able to come home to his warm bed and the welcoming arms of Shelby. Shelby kept herself busy reading about the stages of her pregnancy and preparing a nook in the little cabin for a crib and dressing table for their baby. When they had the opportunity, they visited their families and also spent time visiting Nancy who was a family friend of Chris and Mary's and had a campsite in the same campgrounds they lived at. Nancy was very jovial and it was evident that Todd had known her and her husband for a long time. Unfortunately there was an unspoken uneasiness between Shelby and Nancy. Shelby was rarely included in their conversations and she also noticed that Nancy's smile seemed to be forced. But Shelby never mentioned her uneasiness to Todd; he would have just told her that she was imagining it anyway. So she smiled, tried to enter into the conversations when she could, and began to look at the visits as an opportunity to break the solitude of her life in the cabin.

In late spring Shelby gave birth to their beautiful, healthy daughter. They were overjoyed at her arrival and Shelby discovered what she had always instinctively known, that she loved being a mother. The arrival of Hayleigh filled Shelby's empty hours with the joy of caring for this precious child.

Shortly after Hayleigh was born, Todd graduated from the police academy. He had excelled in the program and Shelby was extremely proud of him. Although he still worked nights and weekends, he was able to spend more time during the day at home with them. They started to socialize with other officers he had come to know at the police department and their families. After a year of marriage, Shelby was still blissfully in love and content in her life with Todd.

As spring turned into summer, Todd learned that his sister and brother-in-law had decided to build a new home. That meant that the house they had been living in, which was owned by his grandfather, was going to be available to move into in a few months. This was welcome news because even though they had enjoyed living in the little cabin, they were quickly outgrowing it. All the items needed for the new baby made the rooms cramped and toys were scattered throughout the house. At one time, everything had a place, but the places to put things had disappeared and the clutter seemed to make Todd edgy every day when he came home.

Just as the leaves were starting to fall, they moved into their new home. They were lucky that Todd's mother had just bought a new dinette set for herself and had graciously given them the old one. His sister left the ancient, but still working washer and dryer and Shelby's sister, who was moving out west, gave them her coffee and end tables for the living room. All that left for the moment was the need to buy a couch, which they bought from a local catalog company.

Shelby loved looking through catalogs and had searched all of them until she found a dark brown sectional sofa. It looked like it would be comfortable and that it would give them and their guest's room to sit.

Soon after moving into their new home, Todd and Shelby started to realize that the costs of raising a child and running a household were more expensive than the meager wages he was earning, so they decided she should go back to work. The good part of Todd's work hours was that he would be home most days to help care for Hayleigh and on the days he needed to work, Shelby's mother had agreed to watch her granddaughter. Shelby quickly found a job at a local fast food restaurant and although it was only a part-time job, it helped with the expenses. Through the months, Shelby and Todd grew more and more at ease with their hurried good-byes as they took shifts working and caring for Hayleigh. She was a beautiful, bright and inquisitive child and filled them with joy. On her first birthday they had a large party with family and friends. The children played games while the adults visited with one another.

These get-togethers were so enjoyable. Shelby loved organizing parties and putting the small touches on these gatherings that made them so special. They weren't able to have them as frequently as she liked due to Todd's work schedule, but on special occasions or holidays she made it a point to get the families together. There was a time when Shelby had pushed her family out of her life. Now, Shelby embraced them all, including Todd's family. They had all been so supportive and caring.

At summer's end, when the air was hot and humid, Shelby started feeling tired. She was having a hard time keeping up with her rambunctious daughter, her fast-paced job, and the normal everyday chores in her home.

As the day of her menstrual cycle came and passed, Shelby realized why she had felt so exhausted. She didn't need the obstetrician to tell her what she expected was the matter, but she verified it just to be sure. She was pregnant; their second child was due in early spring. When Shelby got home from the doctor's office, Todd couldn't help but notice the smile on her face.

"Hey, you look like the cat that ate the canary, what are you so happy about?"

Shelby walked up to him and wrapped her arms around his neck. "Have I told you lately how much I love you?"

"I love you too, but there's something you're not telling me, what is it?"

"You're going to be a daddy again."

Todd's expression was a mixture of shock and pure joy. He pulled her towards him to hold her tightly, then tilted back his head and laughed. "I guess I'd better get a second job hadn't I?"

* * *

Chapter Eight

Todd did find extra work. On occasional weekdays, when he didn't have to work, he took on odd jobs roofing and painting with his cousin Bud. This was a Godsend as Shelby had terrible morning sickness and it became too difficult to work around food all day. She was forced to quit her job. By the end of the second month of her pregnancy, Shelby was relieved that her queasiness and nausea had all but disappeared. She still tired easily but she was delightfully happy to be expecting another child and also being able to stay home and share each day with her beloved Hayleigh.

On a relaxing evening, after eating the dinner that Shelby had painstakingly prepared, Todd said with satisfaction. "That really tasted great Shelb. I don't know where you got the recipe for that homemade spaghetti sauce you make, but it really tastes delicious."

"Why thank you honey." Shelby said cheerfully. "I actually think the secret is the fresh tomatoes I canned this year. They seem to have such good flavor. We were lucky that mom and dad had bushels of them in their garden. I think we have enough canned to last us until next summer. You know, I feel kind of bad that I'm not working and helping with the bills. That's why I canned so many fruits and vegetables this year. Hopefully it will save us some money on our grocery bills."

"I'm sure it will," Todd said more seriously. "But, despite the fact that it's been a little hard on us financially since you stopped working, it's really been great having you home full-time. Hayleigh is so happy you're here, and everything is more organized and seems to be running so much smoother. Besides, even though I hate to admit it, you're a lot better with Hayleigh than I am. It's been sort of nice having a break from watching her. You know I love her with all my heart, but I don't seem to have the patience you have. I just think she's better off being with you."

"Geez, you better cut it out or you're going to make me blush," Shelby said, slightly embarrassed. Todd had never come right out and told her that she was a good housewife and mother before. She turned her head and smiled as she carried the dirty dishes to the sink. "I just love being here, taking care of Hayleigh." Then, Shelby couldn't help but lightheartedly add. "I also know you like working the late shifts, when all the action happens. We both know you weren't able to work that shift very often when I was working and you were watching Hayleigh. It looks like my being able to stay home for a while is working out good for both of us."

"It's that obvious that I like working the night shift better, huh?" Todd said, feeling a little embarrassed himself. "Not only has it been great being able to work the night shifts, but I've been able to put in for extra shifts and get some overtime since I don't have to rush home. That overtime is really helping the paycheck. Between the overtime and the extra money I'm making while working with Bud, we're doing just fine."

Todd working with Bud had also given Shelby the opportunity to meet his wife Bridget who was also pregnant with their second child. Their son was the same age as Hayleigh. Shelby and Bridget became fast friends and the families became very close. Bridget also worked evenings and weekends as a waitress so the schedules of the two families were on the same time frame. Shelby and Bridget got together a few times a week which gave the kids a chance to play. The two couples also got together at least one evening a week to play cards or even go places together like fishing or to the park with the kids.

It was in the middle of Shelby's third month of pregnancy, while sitting at the dinner table, that she noticed that Todd seemed to be very fidgety. Shelby was just about to ask him what he was so antsy about when he blurted out.

"Hey Shelb, I had this really great idea." He was so excited, that he could no longer stay seated. He got up quickly and started pacing around the kitchen.

He had a twinkle in his eye and a smile on his face and Shelby found Todd's excitement contagious. She couldn't wait for him to tell her what his great idea was.

"Why don't you call your sister and see if we can visit for a few days?" he quickly asked. "I could use some of my vacation and personal time from work and we could go out to Las Vegas. Wouldn't that be fun?"

Shelby had just finished preparing Hayleigh's dinner plate and was placing it on the tray of her high chair when Todd said this. She looked up at him, completely surprised and almost stunned.

"Where in the world did you come up with that idea?" she said in amusement, presuming he was joking.

Shelby's older sister Sandy and her new husband Rick, along with her children, had moved to Las Vegas right after Hayleigh's first birthday. Before they left, Sandy and Rick had made the off-the-wall comment to feel free to come visit them anytime, but Shelby had never expected to actually go.

"I've been thinking about it for a couple weeks," he confessed. "We could get away for a few days and while we're there, I can check to see if there are any jobs available."

"Todd!" Shelby said in exasperation. "We can't afford to go to Las Vegas. Even if we did stay at Sandy's, we'd have to buy airline tickets to fly out there. We don't have any money for three plane tickets!"

"No, no," Todd said quickly, as if she had mistaken something he'd said. "We could have your parents keep Hayleigh and then just the two of us could go. Coming up with the money isn't any problem, I'll just borrow it from Chris." His voice was filled with excitement and there was a hint of pleading like a youngster trying to convince his parents that buying a certain toy is a good idea.

Shelby tried to reason with him. "But Hayleigh's never even spent the night at moms; we can't just drop her off and leave her there. Besides, mom has only watched Hayleigh for a few hours at a time, maybe she won't want to keep her for that long."

"Your mom loves Hayleigh, she won't mind keeping her. Just ask her, okay?" Todd said persuasively, not wanting there to be any chance of this trip not occurring.

Shelby could see that she wasn't going to be able to dissuade Todd. He was determined to fly off to Vegas. She couldn't imagine leaving Hayleigh for one night, let alone for a few days, but she couldn't come up with an argument against at least asking her mother if she would mind taking care of her. Maybe she would say no, or maybe Chris wouldn't lend Todd the money, then she wouldn't have to worry about any of it. She could only hope.

Unfortunately, everyone was more than happy to help. Chris assured Todd that loaning him the money wouldn't be any problem; in fact, he wanted to send along some extra money for Todd to throw in the slot machines for him.

Shelby's mother was initially a little nervous about keeping Hayleigh, but just as Shelby let out a sigh of relieve, her mother quickly forgot her hesitations and said she would love to have her.

Shelby couldn't explain her hesitancy about going on this trip. She should have been jumping up and down with excitement at just the thought of going. They could treat this like the honeymoon they never had, couldn't they? And, wasn't she the one who always said, if something is meant to happen, it will? All of the arrangements for the trip seemed to be falling into place so easily, it was a sure sign that they were destined to go. So, was it just the separation from Hayleigh that was bothering her? Or did Todd's sudden idea and insistence that they go to Las Vegas, make her look on the trip with chagrin?

The only thing left to do was to call Sandy and see if it would be all right if they came out. There wasn't any doubt in Shelby's mind that her sister would tell them they could stay with her, but that was her only hope left.

Maybe she wouldn't have been quite so hesitant about going if at least Hayleigh were going with them. The thought of being so far away from her, was just hard for Shelby to imagine. Even though they would only be gone a few days, Shelby was completely devoted to caring for Hayleigh and she knew it would feel more like a few months.

Regardless of how hard Shelby wished all the plans would fall through, two weeks later, they were on their way to Las Vegas. Todd had bought the airline tickets at a nearby travel agency, and Shelby had reluctantly left Hayleigh with her mother. The trunk and inside of the car had been virtually overflowing with toys and everything else that Shelby thought Hayleigh might need. She had written out a page of instructions for her parents and had gone over them one by one so Shelby was sure everything would be done just as if she were there.

Shelby's mother was snickering as she all but pushed her out the door saying. "I have taken care of a few babies in my life Shelby. Go ahead and get out of here, everything will be just fine."

During the flight, Shelby thought about Hayleigh. She already missed her terribly and couldn't believe she had let Todd convince her to go on a trip without taking her baby along too. But, she decided, she might as well enjoy this trip and the chance to go on a vacation with Todd. They would have two children soon and they probably wouldn't be going on another vacation for quite some time.

After the plane landed and they disembarked, it didn't take them long to realize that they had overdressed for the mid October weather of Las Vegas. The cold, damp and dreary weather at home had been replaced with sweltering one hundred and fifteen degree heat. Here they were, dressed in jeans and heavy sweatshirts, while everywhere they looked, more skin could be seen than clothes. They felt like country bumpkins and couldn't wait to gather up their luggage and get out of the airport.

Shelby was so moved when she saw her nephew and niece running towards her. Their arms were opened wide and they were smiling broadly. She loved them dearly. She had babysat them frequently through the years and even though they were eight and twelve now, Shelby held their hands tightly as they waited for the luggage.

As Shelby looked at her sister, she couldn't help but notice that Sandy looked happier than she had in a very long time. Sandy had always been beautiful. Now, with her thick auburn hair pulled back into a long pony tail, her smile a mile wide, and her trim sensuous body molded into her tight shorts, she looked ten years younger than Shelby, instead of ten years older. The move out west had definitely been good for her. Rick looked and sounded the same as always, with his broad shoulders, his ready smile, his booming voice and his hands, moving expressively as he welcomed them. They were gracious enough to quickly take Shelby and Todd back to their apartment so they could change their winter clothing into something more appropriate for this summer weather.

Shelby and Todd couldn't afford to go to any of the shows or to fritter away money at the blackjack tables, but they did spend that first evening out with Sandy and Rick playing the nickel slot machines. Even though they didn't win any money, they had a lot of fun. It had also been fun for Shelby to wear one of the sexy dresses her sister had on hand for when she went out on the town. Shelby had never owned anything that elegant. She wouldn't have had any need for it or a chance to even wear something like that back home. Fortunately Shelby wasn't far enough along in her pregnancy to be showing yet, but, her breasts were definitely fuller. In fact, she had actually lost a great deal of weight because of her morning sickness and lack of appetite so her tall frame was slim and curvaceous. Sandy also had an extensive make-up case as she was a cocktail waitress in one of the casinos on the strip and Shelby had fun, in essence, playing dress-up. Shelby felt and looked as glamorous as any of the other women they saw when they were out. Todd seemed quite pleased with how she looked too. He didn't lavish her with compliments, but then, he really didn't need to. The smoldering looks he gave her along with his attentiveness and the possessive arm he had wrapped around her waist, were enough to convince Shelby that he was enjoying her new look.

The only glitch in the Las Vegas nightlife was that Shelby still tired easily and couldn't stay awake until all hours of the night. So, when on the second night they were there, Todd mentioned that Rick had asked him if he wanted to meet up with him at the casino where he worked, Shelby was actually relieved that she hadn't been included in the invitation. Todd had implied they might be out a little later than she would be comfortable staying up and wondered if she minded if he went without her. Shelby didn't mind at all. She knew Rick didn't get done work until 9:00, so if they were to hang around the casino for a while, and have a couple drinks they might not be back for a couple hours after that and she definitely couldn't stay up that late.

Todd was antsy that evening and couldn't stand sitting around all evening waiting for Rick to get done work, so he took off for the casino at about 7:00. After Todd left, Shelby sat on the living room floor with Samantha and Allen, her niece and nephew. They had planned out everything they were going to do. The kids were thrilled that she stayed home and spent the evening with them. They were usually home by themselves on Thursday's as that was one of the evenings when both Sandy and Rick had to work. Sandy was good friends with her neighbor and had her check on the kids constantly on evenings when she was scheduled to work the same night as Rick.

Before she began her action packed evening with Samantha and Allen, Shelby called her parents to check to see how Hayleigh was. She had wanted to call them several times a day, but kept it to one phone call during the evening. Shelby's heart always fluttered with emotion each time her mother put Hayleigh on the phone.

Hayleigh knew her mother's voice and always cried out "ma, ma" when Shelby started to talk to her. Shelby loved her daughter and it made her happy to hear her voice, but the thought of her not being there with her nearly broke her heart.

After she was assured that everything was fine with her daughter, Shelby and her niece and nephew played a board game and a few games of cards before the kids reluctantly went to bed. They had to be up bright and early in the morning to go to school.

Shelby herself was in bed before 10:00 and as usual lately, she was so tired that she went to sleep quickly. She slept soundly until Sandy's cat jumped on the bed sometime later. She grumbled and shooed the purring cat away. She rolled towards the middle of the bed, intending to snuggle up to Todd, only to find the space where he slept, empty. She rolled back over to look at the alarm clock to see what time it was, and was shocked to see that it was after 3:00 in the morning. She was suddenly wide awake. She had no idea that Todd planned to be out this late. In fact, as she thought about it, he did seem evasive about where he and Rick were going, and what time they planned on getting home. She now wondered whether he had taken advantage of her early bedtime to plan an excursion that she would be excluded from going to.

With each minute that ticked away on the clock thereafter, Shelby's mind ran wild with possible scenarios of what he might be doing. She worried, wondering if they had been in an accident and then she started getting outright angry, wondering if he was with a cocktail waitress like the one he had feverishly admired the previous evening when he didn't think Shelby was paying attention. It wasn't that she wanted to jump to any conclusions or even think in that direction, but she was tired and her hormones were all screwed up due to her pregnancy, so she just wasn't thinking clearly.

Shelby didn't even know whether or not Sandy was with them. She worked nights too, so maybe they all decided to go out together since they knew Shelby was home with the kids. They were probably all playing the nickel slots, were on a winning streak and just decided to keep playing in the city that never sleeps.

By the time Todd came through the bedroom door at 5:45 that morning, Shelby was frantic with fear and anger. She began crying as he walked towards the bed. Todd didn't look at her; his eyes avoided hers as he got undressed and climbed into the bed. He didn't say hi, he didn't apologize for being out so late and he did nothing to sooth and reassure her. Todd simply grumbled that he was tired and needed to go to sleep. His head dropped onto his pillow and he turned so that his back was towards her. Shelby could smell the strong odor of beer and there were other smells emitting from him too. It was a mixture of sweat and sweet perfume.

Shelby laid silently, the tears flowing freely down her face as she tried to still her racing mind. But, she couldn't, so she crawled slowly out of bed, her tears dripping off her chin. She was heartbroken. After putting on her robe, she walked towards the bedroom door. As she started to open it, she heard the cheerful voices of her niece and nephew in the kitchen getting ready to go to school. She took a deep breath and wiped the tears from her face. She would not drag them into whatever was going on between her and Todd. She left the bedroom and ducked into the bathroom across the hallway. She splashed cold water on her face and readied herself to go wish the kids good morning with a smile on her face.

Fortunately, as Shelby entered the kitchen, the kids were heading for the door on their way to catch the school bus. School started and finished a lot earlier in Las Vegas than it did at home. She hugged each of them and told them she'd see them later.

When Shelby walked into the kitchen, Sandy was standing in front of the sink, rinsing off the breakfast dishes and loading them into the dishwasher. She glanced towards Shelby, and smiled weakly as she wished her good morning. Then she quickly announced that she was going back to bed for a while.

Shelby didn't ask her if she had just gotten home too. She wasn't sure if it was because it just didn't seem to matter or whether she was afraid of what the answer would be. She sat at the table, had some toast and juice, and then slipped quietly back into the bedroom to get some clothes to wear. A part of her felt like slamming and banging around inside the room to wake Todd and express how hurt and angry she felt. Instead, she tip-toed as she habitually did while he slept. She knew that Todd didn't like his sleep disturbed so she was used to making sure everyone and everything in the house was quiet. She got her clothes, softly closed the bedroom door behind her and went in to take a shower. Afterwards, she retrieved the newspaper from the front porch and took it out on the patio to read it. It was while looking at the classified section that she realized that Todd hadn't even looked at the help wanted ads since they'd arrived, let alone checked into any leads or set up any interviews. *What happened to coming here to see if there were any job openings he'd be interested in? Was that just an excuse to come out?*

Shelby was so disillusioned that she hung her head and started to cry again. What was going on? She was so tired from being up half the night that she folded the paper and went inside to lie on the couch. She was exhausted and distraught and didn't want to even think about this any more. She knew that everyone else in the apartment was sleeping and that they wouldn't be up for at least a couple hours, so she decided to take a nap.

Mid morning, as Shelby woke, she heard loud voices coming from her sister's bedroom. She couldn't hear what was being said, nor did she want to hear. She got up off the couch, grabbed a few magazines from the coffee table, grabbed her sunglasses off of the kitchen counter and then slipped her feet into her sandals. She wrote a note for Sandy, telling her that she was at the pool and quickly left the apartment.

Shelby was the only person at the pool all the time she was there. She lay in a lounge chair, underneath the umbrella and alternated between mindlessly skimming through the catalogs, thinking about how much she missed Hayleigh and sleeping fitfully.

If Todd was up, he hadn't made any attempt to come out and talk to her. Shelby told herself that she didn't want to hear anything he had to say anyway, so it didn't matter whether he came to explain things to her or not.

At about 2:00, Shelby's niece and nephew arrived at the pool, home from school and ready to swim. They wanted her to go back to the apartment and change into her suit so she could come in with them but, she told them she was feeling too tired today and that she would enjoy just watching them. That seemed to pacify them and Shelby was actually thankful they came out. Seeing them frolic in the pool, dive and do summersaults off the diving board and swim around like fish, distracted her and even made her smile. When they finished swimming, they each grabbed one of Shelby's hands and walked back to the apartment with her. Shelby figured that as long as she could focus all of her attention on the kids, she would be fine.

When they went into the apartment, Todd, Rick and Sandy were sitting around the kitchen table drinking coffee. The atmosphere was tense and quiet. Shelby avoided any eye contact with Todd and went directly to the living room. While the kids were changing out of their swimsuits, Shelby sat up the board game she had promised to play with them. A short while later, Sandy yelled into the living room for everyone to come eat. She had made homemade minestrone soup. Shelby suddenly realized that she was starving, she hadn't eaten since breakfast. She went to the kitchen, filled her bowl and carried it back into the living room so she could eat at the coffee table. Todd followed her in and sat down beside her. He started making small talk and tried to make light his being out all night. There was some mention of drinking more than he should have and that Rick had shown him some of the downtown hangouts frequented by the locals.

Shelby wasn't paying very close attention to what he was saying and wondered to herself whether he actually thought laughing about this would make it all okay. Just then, Shelby heard Sandy's voice coming from the kitchen. It was elevated and had the undertone of anger in it. There was a comment made about topless bars and right away, Shelby knew she didn't want to hear any of this. She stood up and carried her dinner out on the patio so she could eat by herself. She swirled the soup around in the bowl with her spoon as she fought to hold back her tears.

She had a strong feeling in her gut that wherever Todd had gone during the night and whatever he had done, it was something that he shouldn't have. Worse still, was that he would have known it was wrong, would have known that it would upset her, and he had done it anyway.

As she sat on the plane during their flight home from Las Vegas the following morning, Shelby realized that she would never know what Todd had done that night. The saying that 'what happens in Vegas, stays in Vegas' was going to hold true. Todd never apologized for the anguish he had put her through that night. He just acted as though she was making too big a deal about the whole incident.

After they returned home, Shelby turned all of her attention to her beautiful Hayleigh whose sweet smile and warm hugs melted the hurt and anger in Shelby's heart. It took time, but as the weeks passed, Shelby was able to block out the events that happened in Las Vegas and the hurt it caused. This allowed her to open her heart so that she could feel the powerful love she had for Todd once again.

Even though Todd never went out of his way to make up with Shelby, it had been hard for her to stay mad at him. All he had to do was hold her in his arms and tell her how much he loved her and her heart melted. Everyday life seemed to go back to normal. Shelby frequently visited with Bridget and the women grew round with child together. It was reassuring to them both that they had each other for support and encouragement. Shelby knew that no matter what direction their lives led them in the future, she would always treasure these times spent with Bridget.

As neither Todd nor Bridget were around most evenings, Shelby was accustomed to spending quiet nights home with Hayleigh, going to bed early and letting Hayleigh fall asleep beside her at bedtime. She never gave any thought to going out evenings while Todd was working. She had always known how dangerous his job was and knew his attention had to be on what he was doing, not worried and wondering where she was, who she was with and what she was doing. It was out of respect for him and his job that Shelby had decided that she just couldn't be like some of the other police officers wives who went out drinking while their husbands were working. She never wanted to be the cause of him feeling any uncertainty or pain. She had always tried to build his self esteem and confidence as well as sooth, comfort and support him when she instinctively felt he needed it. Sometimes she wondered why he seldom returned those loving gestures, but she would quickly shake the thought from her mind. She knew he loved her and accepted the fact that he just didn't know how to show it.

Shelby also readily admitted, that staying home evenings with Hayleigh was not a hardship, she enjoyed every minute she had with her. Watching her grow and learn as well as sharing laughs and hugs filled Shelby's heart and soul with joy and fulfillment. The thought of another baby being on the way that would need her love and care only increased her joy and also made this time alone with Hayleigh extra special. Her attention would be divided soon, but Shelby knew she had plenty of love in her heart for each child. She rubbed her hand over her swelling stomach and couldn't wait for the arrival of this child.

As Shelby came closer to her due date, Todd's work schedule became busier. It seemed that he either needed to be at court or at a departmental meeting several times a week. That time along with the hours he spent doing odd jobs cut down on the time he was at home. Shelby missed him terribly and complained about it. At one point she took off her wedding ring and hung it in his police car, telling him that he was married to his job more than he was to her. But as always, he would be forgiven for everything as soon as he pulled her into his arms and told her how much he loved her. Todd would again explain to her how much he loved being a police officer and how important it was for him to succeed at it. He would convincingly explain that he wanted to make himself available for any job or detail that was available so that the department would come to depend on him and see how dedicated a police officer he was. He would go on to say how much he missed her and Hayleigh and that he wished he could spend more time with them too, but he needed to be able to do what he needed to do to advance in his career.

Shelby knew all this; she just loved him so much and missed him so much when they were apart. She was also a little nervous as she was close to her due date and she wished he were around more in case she went into labor. Shelby kept herself busy with Hayleigh and painted the bedroom that the toddler would move into when the baby was ready to move into the nursery. She had no doubt that the baby would sleep in the basinet right next to her bed for the first few months, but at least the nursery would be ready and waiting when the time came for the baby to move into it.

On a bright spring morning, Shelby woke up to a strange sensation. Her back was pressed against Todd with his arm wrapped around her huge belly and his face nuzzled in her hair as it normally was, but, instead of being comfortable, her lower back ached and there was a strange tightness in her stomach. Could she be in labor? Her due date was only days away, it was very possible that it was time. Shelby unwrapped Todd's arm from around her and slowly maneuvered her body so that she was sitting up. As she rose, she felt the tightness in her stomach again. When she laid her hand on her stomach she could feel how hard it was. She instinctively knew it was time. She sat back on the bed and gently woke Todd up to tell him.

"Todd, hey honey, you need to wake up."

Todd moaned and rolled onto his back. "How come?"

"I think I'm in labor."

Todd's eyes opened widely. "You sure?"

"I'm not positive but it feels like I'm having contractions. We'd better get Hayleigh to moms just in case."

"Yeah, we'd better go. You go get ready and I'll get Hayleigh up and get her dressed."

Shelby kissed him lightly and was relieved when he sat up and drew her into his arms. She was starting to feel a little nervous.

"Hey, we've done this before and it's going to be just fine."

The feelings of his arms around her always seemed to sooth her and give her strength. She smiled weakly, nodded her head and, as she started to rise, she realized Todd had gotten out of bed. He wrapped his arm around her back and waist and helped her stand. Yes, as long as he was by her side helping her, everything would be all right.

Shelby showered, called her mother and double-checked her hospital bag, while Todd woke Hayleigh and got her dressed. Even though it had only been a short time since she had woke, her contractions were getting stronger and closer together. They loaded into the car and drove to Shelby's parent's which fortunately, was on the way to the hospital. Shelby smiled nervously at Louise, and the reassuring smile that was returned gave Shelby additional strength.

"Hayleigh May," Louise said excitedly as she held out her hands. "Come see grandma and we'll go eat some yummy french toast."

Shelby hugged Hayleigh tightly and said lovingly. "You be a good girl for grandma, ok? Mommy loves you."

With one last kiss, she let her toddler down and watched the little girl run to her grandma's waiting arms.

Louise smiled. "Don't worry about her. I'll take good care of her, she'll be just fine," she promised, and then she walked over to hug Shelby tightly and said reassuringly. "Good luck and call me when the baby is born."

Shelby nodded and they headed to the hospital.

Although they were at the hospital within a half hour, Shelby's contractions were strong and two minutes apart by the time they arrived. They were rushed to labor and delivery. Within an hour, Shelby gave birth to their second daughter. Even though Todd had said he hoped for a boy both times they were expecting, Shelby could tell simply by looking at him, that he was overwrought with joy at the sight of another beautiful and healthy daughter. After the baby was on her way to the nursery, Shelby was moved to the recovery room. As she was being wheeled there, she realized how weak she felt and found it hard to even keep her eyes open. She just wanted to rest for a minute. So, she told Todd to go ahead and call everyone to give them the good news while the nurses got her settled.

Shelby lay in the recovery room alone. She was happy about having another daughter, but the baby had come fast and her mind, as well as her body, seemed to be in shock from the ordeal. The nurses rushed in frequently and were kneading her stomach frantically. Shelby didn't understand what they were doing or the urgency in their faces. She had just given birth, her body had been through enough pain, they must realize how much this was hurting her. Shelby thought her hands were shaking but she wasn't sure, maybe she was just tense from the pain the nurses were inflicting on her as they kneaded her uterus. Another nurse came into the room with a blanket and as it was laid on top of her, Shelby could feel its heat. She couldn't remember ever feeling anything as wonderful as this in her life. Her muscles relaxed and her eyes closed in comfort.

When she awoke, Shelby could feel the soft grip of a nurse's hand and a tug as her body was being transferred from the gurney to a bed. She noticed that she had an IV in her arm and as the nurse covered her, Shelby looked up at her questioningly.

"You're in your room now," the nurse said gently. She gave Shelby's shoulder a reassuring pat. "You gave us a little scare back in the recovery room. Your uterus wouldn't contract so you started hemorrhaging and went into shock," she explained as she fussed with the sheets. "We finally were able to get your blood to clot and the fluids and heated blanket brought you out of shock."

"Is Todd here?" Shelby said, shaken by what the nurse had just told her.

"No," the nurse said hastily. "He must have left while we were taking you to the recovery room, but we've left your room number at the desk so when he comes, he'll know where you are."

Shelby thanked the nurse, trying not to relay her overwhelming feeling of confusion and fear. She desperately needed Todd here by her side, but he had deserted her and left quickly to celebrate the birth of their new daughter. How could he have left the hospital without checking on her and their daughter first?

After taking her temperature and blood pressure, the nurse, looking at her with sympathetic eyes said. "Why don't you rest for a while and then we'll bring your baby in?"

Shelby did still feel weak and very tired. She closed her eyes and let all of her confusion about Todd fade away. She replaced those unsettling thoughts with thoughts about the beautiful daughter that she had just given birth to. She couldn't wait to hold her. When Shelby woke up, Todd was sitting at her bedside smiling.

"Hey it's about time you woke up, how are you?"

Shelby looked at the handsome face of her husband and her heart ached. How she loved this man, and here he was, at her side, holding her hand, with a smile on his face that made him look so happy and proud.

"Hi," she said. Although a smile slipped easily and naturally onto her lips, she had so many questions swirling around in her head that she wanted to ask him. *Where were you? Why did you leave the hospital so quickly? Couldn't you tell something was wrong with me? Don't you care that I could have died?* But, Shelby didn't ask the questions out loud. She didn't like bringing attention to herself and she knew she would end up sounding insecure and pitiful. Besides, she was fine now, so she simply lowered her head and said. "I'm okay".

Then, as if almost an afterthought, her eyebrows rose and she raised her face so that she was looking at Todd. Her excitement was rekindled by the thought of her newborn daughter as she asked. "Did you call everyone and tell them we had the baby?"

"Yeah, everyone was glad you were both doing well. I stopped to see Hayleigh too. Your mom said to tell you that she's fine."

"That's good. Have you seen the baby?"

"Yeah, I stopped by the nursery after I got here. She was sleeping."

"What are we going to name her?"

Todd's crooked smile peeked from behind his mustache. "Well, since you get to have the babies, I should be able to name them. How about Jonelle?"

"I'll gladly let you have the babies anytime you want," Shelby said wearily. "I like Jonelle. That's one of the names on our list."

Two days later, after the nurse wheeled Shelby and Jonelle Lynn out of the hospital, Todd drove them to Shelby's mother's to pick up Hayleigh and then they continued on home. Shelby couldn't have been happier, she now had two beautiful little girls to love and care for.

* * *

Chapter Nine

Shelby reflected how extremely happy and fulfilled her life was with her children. She received so much unconditional love from her little ones. It was a feeling that she could never remember experiencing before. And in return, the love she felt for them was beyond anything she had ever dreamed imaginable. Shelby never felt overwhelmed with caring for her two babies. She only felt the satisfaction a mother feels when ensuring that their child's every need is taken care of and that they are happy. Shelby was more than content to let her life revolve around the girls and Todd.

Todd was more and more engrossed with his duties as a police officer. Shelby continued to support him completely and encouraged him in any steps he felt he needed to take to grow within the department. In essence, she took care of the household chores and care of the children to allow Todd the freedom to pursue every avenue available to succeed in his career. Todd made himself very visible in the community, working at bike rodeos, wearing the McGruff costume to social events and he drove the patrol car in parades. He volunteered his services and attended any additional events he could to show his eagerness and willingness to serve the community and therefore earn their respect and admiration. Shelby and the girls were able to attend some of the events he participated in but they stood in the background, watching him with love and pride.

Even when he wasn't on duty, Todd spent a lot of his spare time with fellow officers. He even joined the department softball team. They had games every weekend against other departments on various fields in various towns. Shelby and the girls went to the games with him though many of the other wives did not. The few that did attend didn't have children and they usually grouped together. Shelby watched Todd play from the blanket on the grass next to the bleachers where she played with the girls. Shelby knew that Todd always received compliments about his adorable children and that, in everyone's estimation, they were the perfect couple and family.

Other than going to these games and visiting their friends Bridget and Bud, Shelby and Todd rarely went out. Their finances weren't that strong with Shelby not working and the expenses of two children, so going to the movies or out to dinner along with the cost of a babysitter just wasn't possible. Besides, as Todd worked most nights and weekends, there were very few opportunities for their schedules to coincide with many social events. They just enjoyed spending what time they could as a family going to the park or just playing in the back yard.

While Todd became increasingly well know in the community and his job gave him ample opportunity to socialize and meet new people, Shelby became more isolated, spending most of her time at home with her children. She was happy and content with her solitary existence; it suited her shy and somewhat introverted personality. Todd's world seemed to be steadily broadening while Shelby's world was becoming increasingly reclusive. But to her, the world she lived in was perfect. She had two beautiful daughters who she loved more than life itself and she had a husband that she was still madly in love with.

Life for them in the rural community where they lived was calm and quiet, but less convenient then it had been previously in the small village where she grew up. Here, they had to drive nearly ten miles to the nearest grocery store and had to go to the local post office daily to pick up their mail since there weren't any letter carriers in this town.

On a warm, sunny day in June, Todd had taken advantage of the weather and was mowing the large front yard with the push lawn mower. It was one of the household chores that remained his responsibility as Shelby wouldn't even consider leaving the girls unattended or in a situation where she couldn't hear them if they needed her.

In the back yard, Jonelle sat contently in her carrier seat on top of the picnic table right next to the swing set, while Shelby pushed Hayleigh on her swing. After the little girl tired of swinging, Shelby sat her at the top of the metal slide attached to the swing set. Shelby held Hayleigh's hand while she slid slowly down the slide. Hayleigh waved her little arms high in the air as she laughed with glee. The red metal swing set had belonged to Todd's niece and nephew who had previously lived in the house. Luckily, they had left it behind when they moved. Shelby laughed as she watched Hayleigh squeal with excitement as she excitedly alternated between swinging and sliding. Shelby finally suggested that they play ring-around–the-rosy, and Hayleigh clapped in agreement. They walked over next to the picnic table where Jonelle was, joined hands and began twirling around in a circle as they began their game. Jonelle watched them as she sat contently in her car seat. Every time Shelby and Hayleigh 'fell down' Jonelle smiled.

When Todd finished mowing the yard, he came out back to play with Hayleigh and share this happy time with his family. Shelby sat holding Jonelle, watching Todd throw Hayleigh in the air, catch her, then hug her tightly. Moments like these were very precious as Todd's schedule didn't allow him much time to spend with either Shelby or the girls. Shelby's eyes misted as she watched Hayleigh laugh and look lovingly into her daddy's eyes. When the girl's finally grew tired, Shelby and Todd carried them inside the house. Shelby changed their diapers and laid them down for their short afternoon naps. While Todd sat on the couch, half reading the paper and half watching a baseball game on TV, Shelby made dinner.

Shelby never wanted days like this to end, but as usual, it went by too quickly. Before she knew it, she was cleaning up the kitchen while Todd went to take a shower and get ready for work. As Shelby finished up the dishes and started wiping off the table, Todd walked in to the kitchen dressed in his uniform. The pants were dark green and the shirt was tan. There were patches on each sleeve, pins on his collar and a name badge on his breast pocket. His gun belt was snapped on and the implements of a law enforcement officer were attached to it; the holster holding his pistol, the handcuffs and a club. He looked so handsome as well as authoritative and menacing. He was proud of the uniform he wore and the position he held. As soon as he put the uniform on, his stature changed and his chest swelled with the pride he felt. He bent over and kissed Jonelle softly of the forehead and then picked Hayleigh to spin her around in a circle before bringing her to his chest and hugging her tightly. Hayleigh's little arms embraced Todd as she laid her head on his shoulder. She loved her daddy and although she didn't fuss, she didn't like it when he left to go to work.

"Bye, bye, daddy," she said softly and sweetly.

"Bye, bye, baby. Be a good girl for mommy, okay?" Todd said as he hugged her once more, and then kissed her on the forehead too.

As soon as Todd set Hayleigh down, she was off and running to the living room to play with her toys and it was Shelby's turn to slide easily into Todd's arms as she always did before he left. He held her closely and as he did, Shelby laid her head on his shoulder to relish these last few moments before he was out the door and gone for another night. Shelby was surprised at how the simple act of being held in Todd's arms could still make her feel lightheaded. As they slowly broke their embrace, they kissed softly, murmured I love you and then Todd left. Shelby watched as he pulled out of the driveway and waved shyly as he drove away.

Shelby and the girls played for another hour, but as the girls had spent the afternoon outside playing in the fresh air, they were tired and ready for bed early. Shelby had successfully moved Hayleigh from the crib to her twin bed with the rail attached in her pink bedroom and had moved Jonelle from the bassinet in their bedroom to the crib in the newly painted yellow nursery. Although both girls frequently fell to sleep nuzzled against their mother in Shelby and Todd's bed, Shelby always moved the girls into their respective beds before falling to sleep. Todd was on the 7 p.m. to 3 a.m. shift and usually home by 4 a.m. unless he had made a late night arrest. Shelby left the light on over the stove so he could see when he came in the back door. Normally in their quiet rural neighborhood she left the door unlocked so he wouldn't have to struggle with the keys in the early morning hours. They never worried about anyone breaking into the house, they didn't have any valuables to steal and besides, who would break into a police officer's house?

After the girls were sleeping, Shelby picked up their toys, straightened up the bathroom where towels and clothes lay after Hayleigh's bath and cleaned the scattered towels and clothes in the kitchen from where she had bathed Jonelle. She was tired too, so after she looked in on the girls and made sure they were settled for the night, Shelby took a shower, put on her nightgown and went into her bedroom. She lay on the crisp, cool linen sheets on their bed and started leafing through a magazine her mother had given her.

The next thing she consciously remembered was dialing the phone over and over. She was holding the receiver to her ear, but the phone wasn't ringing on the other end of the line. *Maybe I dialed it wrong. Let me try again. What number did I just dial? Why wasn't Todd answering? Oh, I'm so tired. The phone is so high on the wall. I just want to sit down. My God, I have blood on my hands. Todd, I need you. I don't know why I need you, but I do. Please answer the phone.*

Shelby awoke slowly, groggily; everything appeared blurred, out of focus. The bright lights hurt, so she squinted and raised her hand to her eyes to shield them. It was then that she felt what might be a hat or bandage covering her head and right eye. She looked down and could see that her hand was being held. She had to turn her face to the right to see who was holding it as her vision was obstructed by whatever was covering her eye. It was her brother Lee who was sitting in a chair next to the bed she was laying in.

"Where am I?" Shelby tried to ask; her voice came out as a whispered croak.

"You're in the hospital." Lee edged closer, but his features remained oddly blurred and flattened. "You were hurt last night."

Shelby's body was sore, and her left arm hurt where an IV had been inserted. Her eyes followed the IV from her arm, up the tube, to the bag containing blood that was on the IV stand by the side of her bed. She was receiving a blood transfusion although she had no idea why. She wanted to ask what had happened, but she was too exhausted to ask any more questions, she held her brother's hand and let sleep take her.

The next time Shelby woke, she felt the tight pressure of a cuff on her right arm. A nurse was taking her blood pressure.

"How are you feeling this morning?" the nurse asked warmly as she pulled off the velcro strips of the cuff.

Not knowing what had happened to her, Shelby tried to evaluate how she felt. "My head aches," she said as she raised her hand to her head. Not only did she have a headache, but when she pressed the palm of her hand on the bandages covering her head, it hurt. Even the gentlest touch caused a burst of pain. Shelby was so confused she began to feel panicky as she continued. "In fact, I hurt all over, why?"

The nurse laid her hand softly on Shelby's arm and gently patted her. She spoke with a soothing voice as she said. "The doctor will be in shortly to talk to you. In the meantime, I'll go get you your pain medication. I'll be right back."

As the nurse quickly disappeared from the room, Shelby got the impression that she was trying to escape being questioned. What was so horrible that the nurse couldn't bring herself to explain it to her? Shelby lifted the covers and looked at the places on her body where the pain seemed to be coming from. She was amazed to discover her body covered with dark bruises and scrapes. What happened to her? She thought this might be how you looked if you'd been in a car accident, but she couldn't remember driving anywhere.

As she laid there trying to figure out what might have happened, Todd came into the room. He walked quickly to her bedside, bent over and as gently as possible, kissed her on the lips. Shelby reached for his hand at the same time he took hold of hers. They entwined their fingers and Shelby held on tightly. She looked into Todd's eyes and felt his protective presence. She released the fear and confusion that had been building in her and she began sobbing.

"Oh, Todd, what happened to me?"

"The doctor will here in a minute to explain what your injuries are, but I'll tell you what happened okay?" He hesitated, cleared his throat as if to help him suppress some of his emotions and continued. "You called me at work. Luckily I was at the dispatch desk." He took a deep audible breath. "But I couldn't understand what you were saying. I could barely tell that it was you. I kept asking you over and over what was the matter and I still couldn't make out what you were saying. Then you didn't say anything. You hadn't hung up the phone but you weren't talking either. I handed the phone back to Sgt. Whitney and I told him to keep listening for you in case you came back on the phone. I told him to make sure you knew I was on my way home."

Todd gulped and the grip he had on Shelby's hands tightened; he was visibly shaking. "When I got home, you were sitting on the couch and you were covered in blood. I didn't know what had happened, but I knew you were hurt very bad. I called the ambulance and then called mom to have her come over and help. While I was talking on the phone, you slumped over on the couch. I was so scared. I ran over and laid you down and covered you up with the blanket because it looked like you were going into shock. I ran to the kitchen to get a towel so I could try to find out where you were bleeding from and put pressure on it to help stop it. Just as I started to wipe your head, mom came through the door so I told her to take care of you while I went to check on the girls."

At this, Shelby felt as though her heart stopped beating. The indescribable fear that arose in her made it hard to catch her breath or think clearly as she screamed. "The girls! My babies!" She struggled to rise to go to them. Then Todd was there, looming over her, firmly pressing her back, demanding that she calm down and listen to him.

Her eyes filled with a look of panic so severe that Todd knew he had to immediately reassure her. "The girls are fine, really Shelby, they're just fine," he kept repeating until she settled down. When she finally let her aching body relax back into the bed, he continued in a slow, even tone to try and keep her calm. "They were sound asleep in their beds when I got there. He gave her a long assessing look before taking his hands off her shoulders and pulling away. As he sat on the edge of her bed, he calmly said. "They're at your mom's now and they're just fine."

Shelby started shaking with relief even though she wasn't quite sure if Todd was telling her the complete truth or whether he was just telling her what she needed to hear. She decided she was just going to have to trust him until they let her go home and see for herself.

"But how did I get hurt?" she asked yet again, hoping this time she'd get an answer.

Todd took a deep breath and as he exhaled, his eyes dropped to the floor and his shoulders slumped as he struggled to swallow his emotions and figure out how he could possibly put into words the horror he found when he arrived home that night. "After I checked on the girls, I went into the bedroom. There was a guy passed out on the floor and he was covered with blood. The bed was covered with it too. I was going to shoot him Shelb; I was actually going to shoot him. Just then the ambulance arrived and mom was screaming for me to get the EMT's in there quick. I knew I couldn't worry about him right then, that we had to get you to the hospital fast. As they were loading you in the ambulance, the State Police got there. When I told them what I found, the troopers wouldn't let me anywhere near the guy or the bedroom after that. I ran back into the house to see if mom needed any help with the girls and she said she'd manage just fine and told me to go ahead and follow the ambulance to the hospital. Mom took the girls over to her house. I don't really know all that happened to you Shelby, but he beat you up pretty bad."

Shelby gasped at what Todd was telling her. She was horrified by the story, but felt detached, as if Todd was telling her the gruesome details of a crime scene he had been called to at work. Something like this couldn't have happened to her, could it? She didn't remember any of it. As her mind reeled with thoughts and feeling, she suddenly was struck with embarrassment and fear as she asked. "Was I dressed Todd? Did I have my nightgown on?"

"Yes hon. You had your nightgown on although your underpants had been ripped off." Todd said with an undercurrent of anger in his voice.

"Oh God Todd, did he rape me?" Shelby said, her voice trembling.

Todd knew that he had to contain his penned up hatred and hostility towards this man that had so viciously attacked his wife. He had to try and keep her calm, not expose her to his anger, so he took a deep breath and calmed himself before he answered. "They tested you, but they don't have the results yet. But you're going to be okay Shelby. Everything is going to be okay."

Shelby was stunned by what Todd had just told her. She had been beaten up badly by someone who had just walked right in to her home. Todd held Shelby's shaking hands for a moment longer and then he bent over and held her tightly. She felt his lips on her forehead as he kissed her and tried to comfort her.

"It's going to be alright Shelby," he promised. "I love you."

* * *

Chapter Ten

"Good morning Shelby, I'm doctor Desoto."

The man in the crisp white coat was tall and had a warm smile that helped ease Shelby's shattered nerves. He walked over to Todd and shook his hand then came to Shelby's bedside. "I was on duty when they brought you into the emergency room," he said as he smiled. "You look better today. How are you feeling?"

"My head hurts," Shelby raised her hand to her forehead and frowned. "The nurse just went to get me some pain medicine, other than that I guess I just kind of ache all over," she paused, and then hesitantly said. "Doctor Desoto, Todd told me I was beat up but he didn't tell what all is the matter with me. Why do I have these bandages on my head?" She smoothly ran her raised hand over the bandages that covered her head and eye.

The doctor took her hand in his and Shelby thought his grip felt gentle and comforting. She also seemed to obtain some measure of strength from the firmness of it.

"You received cuts and contusions as the result of being hit with fists. More extensive injuries occurred to your head and eye due to being assaulted with a shovel." He paused for a moment to allow Shelby to mentally grasp what he was telling her. "You have a fractured skull, you received about 140 stitches and unfortunately, I wasn't able to repair the damage done to your right eye. I'm sorry Shelby, it had to be removed."

Shelby gasped and raised the hand that the doctor had been holding, to touch the bandages over her eye. She looked at Todd, and then started crying, her hands were shaking from the realization of what the doctor had just told her. She now only had one eye and would be maimed for life. She was stunned and couldn't even think of anything to say, she just sobbed.

"Shelby," doctor DeSoto said slowly and compassionately. "I'm sure this is all a shock to you, but you are very lucky to have even survived. Besides your substantial injuries, by the time you arrived at the hospital you had lost a lot of blood and were in critical condition. This is the sixth unit of blood you've received," he said as he pointed to the IV. "But, we should be able to take that IV out of you by this afternoon. I understand that you're upset about the loss of your eye, but I had no choice, the optic nerve had been severed. The surgery went very well though and there weren't any other complications. Although you have quite a few stitches, once your hair grows back you'll hardly be able to notice the scars. You're in remarkably good condition for all you've been through, do you have any questions?"

She shook her head; it was hard enough for Shelby to comprehend what the doctor had just told her, she didn't need to hear anything else. She heard the doctor mention something about him checking in on her later, but she really wasn't listening. She had her eye removed, her head was covered in stitches and she had been beat and possibly raped. My God, they had even had to cut off all her hair! She must look like some freak. How would Todd ever be able to look at her after her bandages came off? How could she even look at herself in the mirror? Shelby felt as if the life had drained out of her. She lay back on her pillow and closed her eye as the tears slid down her cheek.

"You told me he beat me, you didn't tell me he tried to kill me," Shelby said as though completely defeated.

Todd was already at her bedside, holding her hands tightly so she knew he was there. "I didn't know how to tell you everything that happened to you honey. The doctor said that it would be better if he told you," he explained in a tone so raw with pain that Shelby had to open her eye and look at him in concern. "Aw Shelb, the important thing is that you're going to be okay," he repeated the words he'd said earlier as if by saying them over and over he'd force them to be true. Then he shuddered, his eyes filled with moisture, and his lips trembled behind his mustache. "I don't know what I would do if I had lost you."

His voice was filled with so much raw emotion that Shelby realized how hard it must have been for him to know what happened to her but not tell her. She squeezed his hands tightly, then released one so she could run it through his hair to try and soothe him. Then, as if she had been struck by lightening, Shelby sat straight up and tensed. She could see her terror reflected on his rapidly paling face.

"What's wrong?" he asked abruptly, leaping to his feet. "Shelby, are you in pain?"

"Todd, if I'm just finding out about my eye now, when am I going to hear what really happened to the girls?"

"Shelby, I told you the girls are just fine, I promise you they are fine. They're at your mom's; you'll be able to see for yourself as soon as you're released from here."

"Todd, I don't believe you, I want to see my babies. Tell them to let me go home now, I need to see them."

Todd sat on the edge of Shelby's bed and held her shoulders.

"Shelby, look at me," he commanded. "The girls are fine. Hayleigh wants to know where her mommy is, she misses you, and Jonelle doesn't like formula very much, but they're fine. They didn't get hurt, they slept through everything. I promise you they're fine."

Shelby lay back on her pillow. She was still shaking with fear, but felt somewhat reassured that Todd was telling her the truth. Just then the nurse came in with her pain medication and a sedative that the doctor had ordered. Within a short period of time, Shelby felt groggy with the lassitude brought on by emotional exhaustion and the effects of the sedative. Just before she closed her eyes, she looked at Todd.

"Please tell them to let me go home Todd. I'm okay and I need to see the girls."

Two days later, despite the recommendation of Dr. Desoto, Shelby was released from the hospital. The doctor had given her instructions on how to care for her wounds and told her to come back to his office in a week so he could remove the sutures. Most importantly he reminded her of the seriousness of her injuries and ordered her to complete bed rest.

Shelby's parents had already insisted that they stay with them for as long as they wanted to, so that she could heal and so that her mother could help care for the girls. Shelby didn't care where she was as long as she had her babies in her arms.

Before she was discharged, Shelby had stood with her back to the wall mirror and held the large hand mirror up so that she could watch as the doctor unwound the long length of bandage that had been wrapped around her head to protect her wounds. Then she watched as each individual piece of gauze was removed from the cuts on her scalp that were puckered with stitches.

Her first moment of shock occurred at the sight of her bald head. Her silky blond, waist-length hair was gone. She felt naked, as if she had been stripped bare, standing exposed and vulnerable in front of Todd and Dr. DeSoto. She felt like covering her head with her hands to hide the nakedness.

After that initial shock, Shelby looked in horror at the dark thread of stitches that covered her scalp. She looked like the Bride of Frankenstein. Like she'd been pieced together and was being held in place by the stitches. There were so many. They ran across the back of her head, behind her ear, along her forehead, and through the eyebrow above her right eye.

That empty space, the place where her eye once was, was swollen, so the full effect of its emptiness wasn't noticeable yet. Shelby looked long and hard at her face, and then, with a deep sigh, resigned herself to the fact that this was her new reality. She decided right then and there that she would just have to deal with this hand that life had dealt her. She had the doctor put a small patch on the eye and a bandage on the wound above it so as not to alarm the girls. Todd brought in a scarf that her mother had sent and the nurses helped her put it over her shaved and rebandaged head. Then she took her time applying her makeup carefully in a vain attempt to hide the bruises that were so visible. When Shelby arrived at her parent's home after being released from the hospital, she wanted to run in and scoop the girls into her arms, but she wasn't able to run yet. Her depth perception and balance were off and she was still quite weak. Todd understood that she wanted everything to look as normal as possible, especially for Hayleigh, so he wound his arm around her waist to support her as she walked up the sidewalk and steps to the front door. Shelby knew that he had already told Hayleigh that mommy had a 'boo-boo' so that she wouldn't be too surprised by Shelby's appearance.

When Shelby opened the door and saw Hayleigh running to her with a smile on her face, all the fear that Shelby still had inside was set free. Shelby couldn't even feel her pain as she scooped her up into her arms and held her tightly. As she hugged her first born, she looked up anxiously, wanting to see Jonelle too. When Louise walked into the hallway with the sleeping baby in her arms, Shelby's heart nearly burst with joy. Her prayers had been answered and her greatest fear dissolved at seeing her daughters healthy and unhurt just as Todd had told her they were.

Hayleigh leaned her head back and brought her little finger up to the bandage on her mother's eye. "Boo-boo," she said as she bent forward to kiss the bandage. Yes, that kiss was going to make her all better. Shelby hugged her daughter again, and then Todd came and held his arms out for Hayleigh to go into. Hayleigh loved her daddy and went quickly to him. Shelby gave him a grateful look, she was just too weak and unsteady on her feet to hold Hayleigh for very long. She relaxed into Todd's free arm when he put it around her again and walked with her into the living room. After she sat, her mother brought Jonelle over to her. Shelby held the baby in her arms, looking at her beautiful, peaceful face. Even though Jonelle was sleeping, she nuzzled into Shelby's breast… she knew her mommy was holding her.

That afternoon, Shelby lay down along-side Hayleigh to take a nap while Jonelle slept in the crib that had been set up for her. A soft sound from the doorway made her look up. There stood her mother, tears streaming down her face as she watched over them. There was a look on the care-worn face that Shelby had no trouble recognizing. Grief was there for Shelby's pain, intermingled with the gratitude that her life had been spared. Shelby hadn't always gotten along with her mom; they hadn't always understood each other. None of that mattered now. Shelby nodded at her mom to acknowledge the unspoken bond that they now shared. No mother wants her child to be hurt. Her mother finally smiled through her tears and silently closed the door. For the first time since the attack, Shelby drifted into a peaceful, natural sleep, secure in the knowledge that just as she had and would do anything to protect her daughters, so would her mother do whatever was necessary to comfort and sooth her.

That night, their first night together since before she had been hospitalized, Shelby turned her face away in shame when Todd came to bed and lay by her side. She had hesitantly removed the scarf to reveal her head that was now covered with the short stubble that used to be her long, beautiful hair as well as all the bandages covering her scalp and eye. She was also self conscious about the bruises that covered her body. Some had started to turn yellow, while most were still a deep purple.

It was a hot night. Too hot to wear the heavy pajamas that Shelby wanted to wear to cover her wounds. Instead, she wore a light nightgown that allowed all of her ugliness to be visible. She quickly pulled the bed sheet up over her in an attempt to hide. *How can he even look at me, I'm hideous.* Silent tears streamed down her cheeks as she worried about what all this would do to Todd's feelings for her. She had always felt that the love she had for him was stronger than the love he had for her, and now she wondered whether he would be strong and compassionate enough to deal with the extensive injuries she had sustained. Just then, she felt Todd gently pull her chin so that she was facing him. Their faces were close and Shelby closed her eye, embarrassed with the way she looked.

"Shelby. Look at me." Todd said softly.

Shelby hesitantly met his eyes.

He wiped the tears from her cheeks and softly kissed her lips. "Don't ever be afraid to look at me. I can tell you're uncomfortable and upset about the way you look to me, but please don't worry, I don't care. I love you and I'm just so glad you're here next to me. I almost lost you, Shelb."

The silent tears that had been running down her cheeks were now running down his too.

* * *

Chapter Eleven

"Of course I want to go back home. I'm feeling a lot better now and we've imposed on you long enough," Shelby said emphatically as she continued to reassure her mother that she was ready to go home. She realized that Louise wanted her to stay with them longer so Shelby wouldn't have to go back to the place where she was so viciously assaulted, but it was time. Shelby had no memory of what had happened, so she only saw it as returning to her home.

"Todd has already painted the spare bedroom and we're going to use that as our bedroom now instead of the other room. The room where I was hurt has been cleaned and repainted. We're just going to close it off and use it for storage. I'm so thankful that we were able to stay here while I recuperated, and I appreciate your help with the girls so much, but I'm feeling better now and it's time for us to go home. We'll all feel more settled once we're back there."

With hugs and tears, Shelby's parents stood on their porch and watched them load into the car for their trip back home. Her father was a man of few words, so although he didn't say anything, Shelby sensed that he was uncomfortable about them returning to the same house and neighborhood where the intruder had so viciously attacked her. The concern in his eyes was easy to read, but he still smiled bravely and reminded Shelby to call if she needed anything at all.

As they pulled into the long driveway, Hayleigh was excited at the sight of her swing set and Shelby knew they had made the right decision to come home.

"You'll like the bedroom," Todd said lightheartedly. "We painted it a light blue."

Shelby looked at Todd with confusion. "Did your mom help you paint the bedroom?"

"No, why do you say that?"

"It's just that you said we painted the bedroom," emphasizing the 'we.' "Who helped you?"

"Oh," Todd said nonchalantly. "Nancy did. She was over at Chris and Mary's visiting one day when I stopped in and when I told her I was going to the house to paint, she said she'd help that's all."

Shelby thought that all sounded very strange. She could see if their good friends Bridget and Bud had helped or any one of their family, but Nancy volunteering to help just seemed unusual. She had to admit it was nice of her to go out of her way to help Todd like that though. As they pulled up to the back door, none of that seemed to matter any more. She was home. It had been a month since the last time she was here, and she was as happy as Hayleigh to be there. It was a struggle to convince Hayleigh to come into the house when she so desperately wanted to swing and go down the slide, but Shelby promised her that she would bring her back out to play after she took a nap.

Shelby walked up the back steps holding Hayleigh's hand and Todd carried Jonelle in her carrier. Shelby had a little trepidation about actually going in. Would she remember anything that happened as she walked through the house? Todd looked at her after he unlocked the door and could tell by the look on her face that she was nervous.

"Are you okay? We don't have to do this if you're not ready."

Todd's presence gave her the strength she needed to get over that initial nervousness and she knew everything was going to be just fine. She smiled to reassure him and said. "Yeah, I'm okay. Let's go in."

Todd sat the carrier holding Jonelle down on the kitchen table. She was sleeping soundly so there was no need to disturb her. Hayleigh ran into the living room where she knew her toy box was and squealed with glee at the sight of the toys they hadn't brought to her grandmothers house. Shelby walked through the kitchen and into the living room. Everything was as she last saw it, neat and tidy. She walked down the hallway and peaked into the bathroom and then walked into each of the girls bedrooms. Their dolls sat lovingly on their dressers just as she had left them and their sheets and blankets were folded neatly in a basket of clean clothes, waiting to be put on their beds.

Shelby turned and walked into the spare bedroom which would now be hers and Todd's. The walls were painted an eggshell blue and there were delicate white curtains hanging on the windows. The wrought iron bed that they once had slept in was gone and in its place was a mattress and box spring sitting on an unadorned bed frame. Without the head and footboard, the bed looked a little bare, but as Shelby walked towards it, she could see that the bed had been made with the spare sheets she had in the hall closet, so it once again felt familiar. There was a new blanket covering the bed that matched the color of the walls and the pillows were fluffy and new. Shelby could see that a great deal of effort had been made to make her feel welcome in this new room of hers. She walked to the closet and found that all their clothes were hanging there neatly as if they had been there all along. Shelby turned with a smile on her face and noticed that Todd was standing in the doorway looking satisfied.

"Is everything okay? Do you like the color?"

"Oh Todd," she said, her heart melting with the love for this man. "It looks wonderful, thank you so much."

She walked over to him and into his opened arms. She laid her head on his shoulder and closed her eyes. She never knew how to explain to him how protected and safe she felt when she was in his arms. It was if his strength transferred to her when they touched. It was that reinforcing hug she received that helped her to take the next step on her tour of their home.

Shelby walked out of the new bedroom and went across the hall to the room where she had nearly died. But, as she laid her hand on the doorknob, she didn't think of it that way. She thought of it as the room that she had shared with Todd, the bed where they had made love so many times and the corner where the children's bassinet had sat. Todd put his hand over hers.

"Are you sure you want to do this?" he asked, his dark eyes searching her face. "You don't ever need to look in that room again."

"But I do, Todd I know you don't understand, but I don't remember anything that happened on that night," she explained. "I thought if I looked in here, maybe it would help me remember what happened ... and why."

Shelby wished she could just move on with her life and not look back to that fateful night, like everyone wanted her to. But, they didn't realize that to her, that one night changed her whole life. Her appearance had been adversely altered and her perception of everyone and everything had a different perspective. She needed to put together the pieces of that night and find out what happened and yes, if possible, why. Until she knew the answers to her questions, she wouldn't be able to have any closure about the assault.

"Maybe its best that you don't remember what happened," Todd said, his voice filled with concern and hesitancy.

"You're probably right," Shelby said as she looked down at his hand that lay over hers. She wanted to assure Todd that she understood his concerns, but at the same time, wanted to help him understand what she was thinking about moments earlier. "When I hear people talk about what happened, and when I look in the mirror at myself, I have so many questions that I don't have any answers to. Something terrible happened to me, and I don't remember anything about it. I just need to try and find some answers so I can make some sense of all this. I need to understand."

Todd must have heard the desperation in her voice and understood that this was something she needed to do. Shelby knew he didn't want her traumatized further by the knowledge of what happened and that it was probably a blessing that she didn't remember. But, she thought otherwise. She needed to know. She took her hand from the safety of his grasp and walked into the bedroom, knowing Todd would follow. Trusting he would be right there for her.

The room was empty except for some boxes that had originally been stored in the spare bedroom. The walls had been repainted a light green and the hardwood floors were shiny and clean. There was no visible sign that anything had happened in there and although Todd backed out of the room quickly, Shelby stood there, looking at every corner of the room hoping to feel or remember something, anything about the night she was hurt. She couldn't though. She thought about the words that were spoken to her that night. "I don't want to hurt you." And she tried to envision their bed in the far corner. She strained to put those words to a face or to what had been done when the words were spoken. But again, there was nothing.

Shelby walked around the room one last time, and then exited closing the door behind her. As she walked down the hallway to return to the living room, she tried to conceive how she possibly got from the bedroom to the phone that was on the wall at the end of the hallway. She could only remember dialing and dialing the phone, not how she got there and not talking to anyone. It was all astonishing to her. How could she have been hurt as badly as she was, lost as much blood as she had and still gotten herself to the phone twenty feet down the hallway to call Todd?

It suddenly became abundantly clear to her that the Lord was by her side, helping her that night. He had delivered her from death.

Her deep thoughts and reverie was broken as Hayleigh ran towards her hugging her much beloved Kermit doll.

"Sweetie why don't you go rock Kermit in your chair while mommy makes your bed, okay?"

Hayleigh smiled, turned and ran to the small wooden rocking chair next to the couch. With a great deal of maneuvering, she backed into the chair and looked lovingly at her small frog as she slowly rocked back and forth. Shelby knew that this would slow her down so she would be ready to take her nap soon. She went back into Hayleigh's bedroom and put the sheets, pillowcase and yellow thermal blanket with the silky edge on the child's twin sized bed. She attached the railing so she didn't have to worry about Hayleigh rolling out, and then went back into the living room to get her daughter. Hayleigh's eyes were watery and drooping, she was indeed ready for her nap. She went readily into Shelby's outstretched arms still holding Kermit. She laid her small head on Shelby's shoulder as they went back to the bedroom. Shelby laid her gently onto the bed and covered her with her blanket. Hayleigh drew the blanket to her face with one hand then nuzzled her face against the green frog that was still clutched in her other hand. She immediately closed her eyes, warm and comfortable in her own bed. Shelby stood at the doorway gazing at her beloved daughter for several minutes.

After she was sure that Hayleigh was fast a sleep, Shelby walked back into the kitchen to get the just now waking Jonelle. She was such a good baby, she hardly ever cried. Shelby loved taking these opportunities when she wasn't running after Hayleigh or doing housework to just hold her baby in her arms. Shelby got one of the bottles she had prepared earlier and as it warmed, she changed Jonelle's diaper. She picked Jonelle up and carried her while she took the diaper to the diaper pail in the bathroom. With two children in diapers, Shelby had tried to economize by using cloth diapers instead of buying disposable ones. It was definitely a lot more work dealing with them, but she tried every way she could to stretch Todd's paycheck. She then went back into the kitchen, tested the bottle to see that it wasn't too hot and walked into the living room to feed and hold her baby. As Shelby had nursed Hayleigh until she was ready to drink out of a cup, she was disappointed that she had had to stop nursing Jonelle after she was injured. Her body had sustained so much trauma and she had lost so much blood that it caused her to stop lactating. Jonelle had eventually gotten used to the bottle and formula but it was important to Shelby that she continue to hold her while she was feeding her so that Jonelle could be in her mothers' arms and be lovingly held against her breast. She cherished these quiet moments when she was able to bond with her second child.

After Jonelle had been fed and lay sleeping on her shoulder, Shelby carried her into the new bedroom and laid her on the bed. She placed a pillow on either side of Jonelle, then went back into the baby's nursery and put the clean sheets on the crib. After she retrieved Jonelle and laid her gently in the crib, she went back into the kitchen and stood watching Todd from the window as he mowed the lawn.

It was impossible for her to know what he was thinking and feeling about returning to this home of theirs. Shelby knew that while she didn't remember any of the horror that had occurred here, he did. He'd found her, he'd seen all the blood, and he'd found the assailant passed out on their bedroom floor. He had also been the one who re-painted the room to cover any reminder of what happened; to shield her from seeing the spattered blood stains that covered the walls. Todd had never been one to talk about his feelings and other than fleeting moments where he let down his guard and allowed himself to show his love for Shelby and his daughters, he'd never been good at allowing himself to show much emotion at all. Shelby had always accepted the fact that he held his feelings at bay and that he could not show his emotional vulnerabilities with her. She was just going to have to hope and trust that he was handling all of this all right.

Shelby went back and peeked into each of the girls' rooms to be sure they were still sound asleep, and then she went out the front door and sat in the sunshine on the patio. She sat down on the edge of the cool cement floor and her legs dangled down so that they almost touched the ground. The steady hum of the lawn mower in the back yard could be heard as Shelby took in the sight of their front yard. The maple and locus trees were lush with leaves and as she looked upward, she saw that the sky was clear and blue.

This peaceful setting should have enabled her to clear her mind and relax. Instead, Shelby fell into the thought pattern that plagued her most of the time now. She reflected on what had happened to her and how she now looked. She ran her hand over her short hair. It was starting to grown back and she was now able to brush her hair so that most of the scars were now hidden. But, she wasn't used to having short hair. She hadn't had short hair since she was in the elementary school and had never learned the fine art of using the blow dryer and curling iron to style it. She knew Todd had loved her long blond hair and she wondered if some of her appeal had been lost when it had been cut. Then she ran her fingers over the scar above her eye and over the patch that still covered what was missing from beneath it. The surgeon had done such a good job; she appreciated the delicate and tedious work he had performed when he reconstructed her eyebrow and ensured that at least her tear duct remained in tack. These small things might not mean anything to anyone else, but to Shelby it gave her some feeling of normalcy.

She would be going to the occularist soon to have a prosthetic eye made. Although it was sometimes difficult for her to look at herself in the mirror, for the most part she just accepted the fact that it was gone. Yes, her vision and appearance would never be the same, she had been savagely beaten, possible raped and then she had been chopped in the head with the pointed blade of a shovel. But, the Lord must still have plans for her as she had survived the assault and more importantly to Shelby, He had protected her daughters from harm. Losing an eye seemed a very small price to pay for the chance to continue raising her children.

But, what did Todd think when he looked at her? Was he just being supportive because it was expected of him? Would he really be able to accept her the way she was now?

"Hey, what are you doing out here?" Todd's voice broke into her thoughts. "I thought you'd be resting while the girls were taking their naps."

"No, I'm not tired and it's so nice out that I thought I'd sit here for a minute. Are you hungry? It looks like there are a few things to eat in the fridge; I'll go in and make you some lunch."

"Yeah, I'm starting to get a little hungry and I could use a big glass of iced tea too okay?"

"Sure." As Shelby got up she looked lovingly at Todd. "Hey, hon, it's good to be back home."

"I know. It was nice of your mom & dad to let us stay with them for a while but it's really nice to be back in our own home."

* * *

Chapter Twelve

It would have been nice for Shelby to think that all she had to do was heal physically from her wounds. But she soon discovered that the physical healing was the easiest part to overcome. The battle she had to fight now was the emotional toll that all of this had taken on her.

Everyday things she once did without a second thought were now agonizing feats which drained her of every ounce of courage that she could muster up. She was dismayed to discover that she was no longer able to take a shower or run the vacuum cleaner unless Todd was home because the noise of the water and cleaner left her unable to hear what was going on around her. She found that she even had to keep the shower curtain slightly open, even after securely locking the bathroom door. She would look around continuously, leery that an assailant was waiting for just the right moment to attack her again. She would become so scared that she felt short of breath and her chest felt like someone was sitting on it. Her hands would shake and she would be covered in a cold sweat. She was sure she was having a heart attack as her heart would race so fast and beat so loudly she could hear the unsteady cadence of it pumping in her ears. She was so afraid that it was all she could do not to scream and would end up crying until she was safely in Todd's arms.

Within a short period of time, this all-consuming fear started to engulf her at the least expectant moments, especially at night. It didn't matter whether she was in the store doing her grocery shopping or whether she was sitting on the couch watching the TV on a quiet evening. All of a sudden her heart would feel like it was skipping a beat, then after what seemed like a minute of no beat at all it would race so quickly Shelby thought she could actually see her heart beating in her chest. This was always followed by the shortness of breath and the feeling that someone was standing behind her with their arms wrapped so tightly around her chest that it squeezed the breath out of her. Her hands would shake and all she could think of to do was call out to Todd.

These debilitating attacks were starting to occur daily. Shelby dreaded them, and even lived with trepidation of the oncoming attacks. Fear began ruling and taking over her life. At least with Todd there nights, she had been able to hide the worst of these episodes from the girls but, she wondered how she would handle the situation when Todd went back to working evenings … which would be soon.

Shelby wished that Todd could just continue to work days like he had been for the two months since she had been hurt. Although she knew it was unrealistic for her to hope that it was even a possibility. Todd had explained to her more than once that only the officers who had seniority were able to work during the daytime hours. For the most part, working night and weekends was just the norm when it came to police work. He had told her several times how they'd been very lucky that his fellow officers were so sympathetic to Shelby's predicament. The department had understood when he'd requested to work the day shift so he could be there for her during the darkness of the night for a while.

Despite the fact that Shelby's wounds seemed to have healed fine, there wasn't any doubt that the psychological scars were becoming overwhelming and obvious to those around her. Even though she needed Todd to be home nights with her more than ever, there was nothing they could do to prevent his return to the night shift. Bud and

Bridget promised to check on her frequently and reassured both Shelby and Todd that they were just a phone call away. Todd's mother and Shelby's parents also gave their full support and repeatedly promised to help Shelby and the girls make it through this tough time in any way they could.

This whole situation was all so disturbing to Shelby. She had once been a very competent person and had been confident in her ability as a mother and wife. Now she was experiencing so much anxiety and doubt that she was having a tough time dealing with even the simplest things. She lived in so much terror, that she never wanted to be alone, and the only tranquility she could ever get was when she turned her full attention to the girls. Taking care of them and making sure they were happy was Shelby's main focus. While she was with them, her protective instinct for them took over and was strong enough to suppress the ever-present fear that filled her. She was miraculously always able to hold off any major anxiety attack when she was alone with her children. The natural maternal instinct she had and her strong love for her daughters seemed to be the only thread that she had to cling to through the darkness of her perpetual fear.

When Todd returned to his regular work schedule, Shelby often got the impression that he welcomed the return to that normalcy. Not only did he seem to thrive on the hidden dangers and actions of the nightlife, but he often seemed to be at a lost when it came to dealing with Shelby's emotional and psychological issues. His time away from home was probably his reprieve just as Shelby's was her devotional and full attention to her children.

Shelby somehow endured the next few months. She had gone to see her physician and he had prescribed Valium to help her relax, especially during the nighttime when the fear seemed to engulf her. Shelby admitted that these helped with the severity of the attacks but she was never fully free of the anxiety all together. In fact, for the most part, while she may have outwardly appeared relaxed, her mind was still filled with terror and she could still feel her heart beating hard and fast in her breast. She knew the cold, clutching fingers of fear still held her tightly in their grasp, but she felt that with the aid of the Valium, she was able to hide most of the attacks from Todd. She no longer wanted him to know what she was going through or how often these panic attacks hit her. He thought of her fear as a weakness and the continuous attacks were starting to take its toll on Todd's patience and sympathy. So, Shelby often smiled and went silently into another room at the onset of an attack. She had learned breathing techniques and had a paper bag safely hidden in the kitchen and under her bed for times when she hyperventilated, which is what the doctor had assured her was happening when she became short of breath and felt like her chest was being squeezed. She was coping with the attacks and she was hiding them from her family as well as Todd. She didn't want to feel like she was a burden to any of them. It seemed to make everyone feel more at ease knowing that she had made it through this difficult time of emotional instability.

As fall and winter arrived, the short days and the long nights of darkness were like a long shadow looming over Shelby. She would close the curtains and securely lock the door at the onset of the darkness. Not only did Shelby shut out the darkness, she also shut off the world outside her door. She rarely went out on any evening even when Todd was home. The fun times spent with Bridget and Bud playing cards or just visiting over coffee with family members came to an end when evening arrived. After the girls were safely in bed for the night, Shelby would find herself in the safety of her own bedroom watching TV until she could no longer keep her eyes open. She never turned the TV off; it was the sound of the voices that broke the silence and reminder that she was alone. She could never sleep soundly either, she was always half listening for any cries from her children like mothers do, and she also listened to ensure that nothing was going on in her home that shouldn't be. Because of this, Todd never came into the house silently as you would expect a person to do in the middle of the night. He always turned on the lights and walked heavily on the wood floors so that Shelby would know that it was him who was entering their home and then into the bedroom. She always heard him and she was always partially awake when he came into the bedroom. He would turn on the light, turn off the TV and then Shelby would hear the familiar and repetitive action of him unbuckling the snaps that held his police belt securely in place, the gun being placed in the upper shelf of their closet and his handcuffs being placed on the dresser. She would soon feel the warmth of his body after he got into bed. They would frequently make love and even during the rare occasion when they didn't, they would still lay with their legs entwined or their arms wrapped around each other. Some part of their bodies would always be touching. She could feel him there, he was home and with that knowledge she was able to finally fall effortlessly into a more relaxed sleep until the girls were ready to rise a couple hours later.

Shelby and Todd had just finished the final session at the occularist to have her glass prosthetic eye made. It was another roller coaster ride for Shelby's emotions.

Although there was no getting away from the fact that she had lost her eye, she faced that reminder in the mirror every morning, for some reason, she hadn't fully accepted the fact that she was actually missing a part of her body. Through each step, from their first consultation to the day her new eye was completed, Shelby had to face the reminder that she was not physically whole and that she needed a man made object to replace the part that was now missing. She learned that the eye would have very little movement and she would have to move her head rather than her eyes when she spoke to people. She also realized that there would never be that gleam of happiness in that eye or the ability to express any emotion other than with tears. On the first visit, the occularist had noted what a skillful job Dr. Desoto had done during Shelby's surgery and was pleased that he managed to save her natural tear duct. Shelby knew she should be grateful, but … the fact remained that she still needed a glass eye. Oh it looked exactly like her other eye, Donna Swanson, a nationally renowned occularist, whose practice was less than an hour's drive from Shelby's home, had done a truly magnificent job creating it. The detail necessary to ensure that the eye appeared real, made the process seem as if it were a science or an art form. The curvature of the eye had to be exact so that the eyelid laid on it in exactly the same position as the real eye. And, the eye was hand painted. The color matched the real eye exactly and placement of miniscule red threading gave it the appearance of having blood flowing through its veins. Yes, the eye was a work of art. Even though Shelby appeared whole and normal again, she would always have this as a reminder of that fateful night when her world was shattered apart.

After receiving the new prosthesis, Shelby made a follow up appointment to see Dr. Desoto. She was due to go back so he could see how her wounds were healing and she knew he would be delighted to see what fine artwork her occularist had created.

Shelby and Todd sat in the reception area waiting to be called in to see Dr. Desoto. As the door to his office door opened, Shelby glanced up to see if she was the one that would be called in by the nurse. To Shelby's surprise, the doctor himself came out of the door with a wide and warm smile on his face.

"Look who's here. Come on back, Shelby."

Shelby had to smile. He made her feel so welcome and at ease. As she walked closer to him he reached out his hands and took hers in his.

"Let me look at you," he said with a gentle smile as his eyes swept over her. "You look absolutely wonderful."

Shelby looked up at him, a smile that changed from sheepish to glowing spread across her face. She had not felt attractive for a very long time, but the way he looked at her, beaming with happiness and pride made her feel special and as wonderful as he said. She could feel his eyes take in hers as if he was indeed looking at a fine piece of art.

"Come on back," he repeated.

They walked through a short corridor and into the examination room. Shelby sat down in a chair that you would normally see at your optometrist's office when getting your vision checked for glasses. It hadn't really occurred to her that this man who had done such specialized work on her, was also someone you could go to see to have a simple vision exam. The first time she had come to his office, she had just gone into a room that looked like any other medical office with its elevated bed, sink and cupboard with medical supplies inside. It was there that he had removed all of her stitches and had told her how remarkably well she was healing.

"Your eye is a perfect match," he said, his voice filled with wonder. "If I didn't know better, I wouldn't know that it was a prosthetic. May I look at it more closely?" he asked almost eagerly.

Shelby nodded her head and sat back as the doctor used all of his equipment to look at the eye up close. She heard him repeat the exclamation "remarkable" over and over and when he was done examining her he simply sat back and smiled.

"Young lady, you look so wonderful, especially after all that you have gone through. I can't believe you're the same person that came into the emergency room. Dr. Swanson has done a wonderful job with your eye and you look great. Is everything else going all right?"

Shelby could have told him about the emotional hell she had been going through, but right at this minute, with those warm eyes and smile looking at her with the same pride a parent has when their child graduates from high school, she felt on top of the world. For the first time, someone was looking at her as if she was beautiful, not as if she were a maimed person who should be pitied. He knew that it was a miracle that she was even alive let alone sitting here as if she were just another patient coming for their yearly vision test.

"Good," he said with satisfaction when she told him everything was fine. "Now you're going to have to take especially good care of your remaining eye. There is always the chance that your eye can become infected from your contact, I am recommending that you wear it only on special occasions and get some eye glasses to wear the rest of the time. They will not only help your vision but they will give you another layer of protection from any injuries."

Although Shelby had always hated glasses and how she looked in them, she trusted this doctor implicitly and knew that the advice he was giving her was something she should take seriously and she agreed to do just that. Dr. Desoto gave her a quick exam and wrote her out a prescription for her lenses. As she left his office, she realized that she probably would never need to see him again and suddenly she felt an intense gratitude for everything that this man had done for her.

"Thank you for everything," she said as she walked toward him. Tears came unbidden to hers eyes, to both of them, including the eye that he had so skillfully left the tear duct in tact. She wrapped her arms around him and they hugged each other with a mutual respect and admiration. It wasn't until she was out in the car after her appointment that she realized that giving your doctor a hug wasn't something a person normally did. But it seemed like the natural thing to do. The man had not only given her the ability to cry, but he'd given her cause to cry in happiness for the first time since the beating. Shelby still wasn't able to drive, her depth perception was off so much and that, together with the loss of vision on her right side, made her a little uneasy about jumping into the driver's seat of the car. She knew that eventually she would feel more confident in her ability, but Todd did most of the driving anyway so she'd deal with it when she needed to. When she told Todd that the doctor had suggested she get glasses he agreed with her.

"You might want to get a tint on the glasses too, and then your eye won't be so noticeable."

Shelby was taken aback with the comment Todd has just made. He said it with such ease. Didn't he realize that he had just told her that he thought she should hide her eye? She would have said something if she could have thought of something to say but his words had stunned her. She had just left a doctor who had beamed with pride over what she had overcome and had stated how natural her eye looked. Now she was listening to Todd tell her she should be hiding beneath tinted glasses. Shelby was suddenly self conscious and unsure of herself. She wondered if that was how everybody felt. Did she make people uncomfortable? Did they want to cringe at how she looked? She decided that Todd was right and it probably was the best idea to get tinted glasses so that the eye was indeed less noticeable.

As long as they were already out, they went to the mall and into the vision center and picked out a pair of glasses with large frames and tinted lenses. No one would ever even know about her eye with these on. With the knowledge that she would now be unobtrusive, Shelby left the mall an hour later feeling reassured by Todd's approval of her choice. The glimmer of self-confidence and attractiveness that she'd felt in her doctor's presence was forgotten and replaced with the comfort Todd's approval always brought.

* * *

Chapter Thirteen

As the holidays neared, Shelby's anticipation and excitement helped mask the fear which still engulfed her. She had made pumpkin shaped sugar cookies with the girls for Halloween and now she and Todd laughed as they watched Hayleigh, looking hesitant, gingerly sink her tiny hands into the 'guts' of the pumpkin that was being cleaned out in preparation for being carved into a jack-o-lantern. Todd had first cut open the pumpkin, pulled the top off, and started scooped the 'guts' out with a spoon. Then, with a devilish grin on his face, he lay down the spoon and reached his hand inside the pumpkin. He used his fingers to grasp the gooey mess then plopped the innards onto the newspaper that Shelby had spread underneath the pumpkin on the kitchen table. All this was done under the watchful eyes of the little girl. With just a little coaxing, Hayleigh reached into the pumpkin to mimic what her daddy had done.

After Hayleigh had her fill of squishing the seeds between her fingers, Shelby chased her into the bathroom where she was given a bath. Meanwhile, Todd finished scraping the pumpkin clean, carved a face into it that had a toothy smile and put a candle into the jack-o-lantern. Soon, Hayleigh ran excitedly back into the kitchen after being washed and her nightgown put on. She was anxious to see what her daddy was doing to the 'punkin' now. Shelby put the clothing that her little girl had been wearing into the hamper and then hung up the wet towel before going into the kitchen where Hayleigh's excited squeals could be heard.

As Shelby walked into the kitchen, she saw Hayleigh joyously jumping up and down, clapping her hands.

"Mommy, look," Hayleigh said as she pointed at the pumpkin. Her face glowed with happiness. She had a smile that seemed to reach from ear to ear and a twinkle in her eyes that seemed to light up the room.

Even Jonelle, who was contently playing in the playpen they had moved to the kitchen, embraced Hayleigh's excitement and began to laugh as she stuck the green doughnut shaped toy into her mouth.

Shelby looked towards the table and saw the completed jack-o-lantern and then looked towards Todd to give him an approving smile. The expression on his face revealed the pride and contentment he felt as he watched his daughter run towards the creation he had made.

Shelby lifted Hayleigh onto the chair beside the table and Hayleigh automatically kneeled on it, so that she was eye level with the pumpkin. Her eyes growing ever larger the nearer she got to the smiling face that sat in front of her. She rested her chin in her hands as she leaned her elbows onto the table edge. Her long, wet wheat colored hair hung neatly down her back. She sat patiently, waiting and watching intently as her daddy lit a match and reached inside the pumpkin. Shelby had walked over and picked up Jonelle so she too could be included in the festivity of lighting the candle in the pumpkin.

As the jack-o-lantern sprang to life, its face aglow from the light within, Hayleigh's little mouth formed an O as she looked in wonderment and surprise at the smiling face shining in front of her. She looked at her mommy with questioning eyes. When Hayleigh saw the amused happiness on Shelby's face she was reassured that the jack-o-lantern was a cheerful anomaly rather than a scary one, and instantly she resumed her animated clapping.

As fun as this was, when the time came for them to go out into the sparse neighborhood to go trick-or-treating, Shelby found that she was too afraid to go out. Shelby apologized to Todd about not being able to go trick-or-treating, and stayed in the safety of her home with Jonelle while he took Hayleigh out with Bud, Bridget and their children. It was only after they had left, that Shelby came to the shamed realization that she was also unable to welcome trick-or-treaters into her home. She shut off the light on their porch that was to be lit if you were participating in handing out candy. The fear of her greeting a masked stranger at the door who might turn out to be another assailant, kept her from the pleasure of watching young children dressed as their favorite cartoon characters innocently seeking candy. With the curtains pulled tightly shut, Shelby sat in the quietness of the living room as Jonelle played with her toys in the playpen, oblivious of her mother's fear. Shelby was ever watchful and listened carefully for any noise that might indicate an intruder coming.

She was overwhelmed with relief when the familiar sound of their car announced the return of Todd and Hayleigh an hour later. She exhaled loudly, purging the lump of anxiety from her aching chest. She greeted them at the back door with her arms extended and a huge smile on her face. Hayleigh rushed into her mother's open arms and then proudly displayed the bag of candy that she had obtained while out trick-or-treating.

"Look mommy, candy," Hayleigh said excitedly.

"Wow," Shelby said, as she peeked into the bag. "Look at all this candy you have. Let's pour it on the table and see what you have in here."

As Shelby inspected the contents that had been in the bag, pulling out candy that Hayleigh was not allowed to have, Todd walked through the kitchen and started down the hallway towards the bedroom.

"Did many kids show up at the house for trick-or-treat?" Todd asked, as he disappeared down the hallway.

"No," Shelby said softly. "Actually, I didn't turn on the porch light." Her voice emphasized the shame and embarrassment she felt as she continued. "I was afraid a teenager or adult with a mask would come to the door and I didn't know what I would do if that happened."

Shelby heard Todd's footsteps coming back down the hallway as he returned to the kitchen. When Shelby looked up, she saw Todd standing in the doorway staring intently at her. The meaning in his eyes couldn't be mistaken. Shelby was sure that he wanted to shake his head in disappointment, but instead he coolly said. "Are you alright?"

"I'm fine," Shelby said as she turned her attention back to the table of candy and sighed disheartenly. "I realize there probably wouldn't have been any problem and I really missed seeing all the kids in their costumes, but I just couldn't chance it."

"Actually you weren't the only one around here that didn't have the light on and there weren't many kids out anyway. We had to go all the way into the village to find enough houses on a street that had their lights on. Luckily, the kids are so young we only had to go down a couple streets and they were happy. Well, if you're okay," he said as he turned and resumed walking down the hallway to the bedroom. "I'm going to go into work for a while. Now that the young kids are off the street, the teenagers will be coming out looking to get into some trouble. I told the chief that I'd be available to work for a few hours after we got back from taking the girls out trick-or-treating. We could use the overtime with Christmas coming up. You don't mind do you?"

How could Shelby say yes, she did mind? He could see that she was nervous, in fact she had just told him so not two minutes ago. She wanted him there so she could relax and feel safe. But she wasn't a whiner and as he was already starting to change into his uniform, what could she say? He would just be irritated with her if she asked him not to go, so she just said. "No, I'll be fine. You aren't going to stay out too late though, are you?"

"No. Probably until eleven or twelve, by then most of the kids should be off the streets and the night shift will be able to handle things."

"Okay," she said, determined to push her panicky feelings aside. "I think after all that excitement it's going to take Hayleigh a little while to settle down anyway. So I'll just play with her and that will keep my mind off everything else."

"If you need anything just call the office and they'll radio me, okay?"

"I won't need to do that," she said confidently. She knew she was trying to convince herself that she would be alright as much as she was trying to assure Todd. "I'm fine now," she insisted.

Shelby watched as Todd gave both the girls their goodbye hugs and kisses before he came to her. He then drew Shelby into his arms and as she wrapped her arms around his neck, he wrapped his arms tightly around her waist. She laid her head on his shoulder, closed her eyes, and again felt strength seeping into her system. As always, being in his arms renewed and reassured her and made her feel protected. They parted slightly, just enough to allow them to kiss passionately while they held each other.

Her fear subsiding, Shelby looked deeply into his eyes. "I love you. Please be careful tonight, okay?"

"You know I will be," he said, his crooked smile peeking through the dark mustache. "Lock the door behind me and I'll see you in a little while."

"Yeah, I'll see you later."

After Todd closed the door, Shelby locked it. He'd barely left her sight and already she was starting to feel the dread of being alone … at night … again. Before she sank completely into that dark place, Shelby's attention was fortunately drawn to her little angel who came racing into the kitchen. Hayleigh was laughing and looking up at her mother with pleading eyes. She pointed to the table and said. "Candy please mommy?"

Shelby had to smile and the dread that had started to seep into her was chased away by the smile and innocence of her beautiful child standing in front of her. "That's just what you need, another piece of candy," Shelby whispered softly to herself. To her eager daughter, Shelby cleverly suggested. "Why don't we save it until daddy's home and then you can share it with him, okay?"

Hayleigh started to protest then a look of glee came into her eyes. "Daddy have candy too?"

"Yes," Shelby smelled victory. "Don't you want to wait and share your candy with daddy?"

Hayleigh nodded cheerfully and as quickly as she had run into the kitchen, she ran back into the living room where Jonelle was still playing contently in the playpen. Shelby quickly put the candy back in the bag and placed it on top of the refrigerator so that it would be out of reach. Then she went into the living room to play with the girls. Although Shelby wished Todd was able to spend his evenings at home with them, she reminded herself that his job made that impossible and anyway, she was blessed with two beautiful children that made the long nights bearable by just being with them.

As Shelby gave Jonelle her bath and rocked her to sleep, Hayleigh played and got the sugar and excitement out of her system. As soon as she started to slow down, Shelby put Jonelle to bed for the night and then gave Hayleigh a warm bath. Afterwards, she took her into her bed and lay down beside her. Hayleigh nuzzled up to her mother and before long the toddler was sound asleep. Shelby quietly got out of Hayleigh's bed and put the rail up so that she wouldn't fall out. She bent over and kissed her gently on her forehead and walked towards the bedroom door. She turned back to look at her daughter who lay sleeping soundly and Shelby was overcome with the feeling of love that filled her each time she gazed upon her daughters. She walked out of the room and went into Jonelle's room to check on her. She too was sleeping soundly. Little angels Shelby thought. They never gave her any trouble and were such a blessing that she didn't know what she would do if she didn't have them to love and care for.

Shelby went back into the living room and picked up the books and toys that Hayleigh had been playing with. She looked in the kitchen to make sure everything had been straightened up, then she went into the bathroom and wiped around the bathtub where Hayleigh had splashed. She hung up the towels to dry and then turned off all the lights, except for the light over the stove and went back into her bedroom. After turning on the TV, she changed into her nightshirt and lay on the bed. She knew it would only be a couple hours before Todd got home, but the minutes on the clock ticked by very slowly during those evening hours. When at last she knew that Todd should be on his way home, Shelby allowed herself to relax so she could fall to sleep. She never really knew exactly what time Todd ever arrived home, but just the thought that he should be returning at a specific time allowed her to let go of the protective shield she had placed around her and her daughters, relax, and let Todd's protective presence take over.

As with the usual pace of the holiday season Thanksgiving was soon upon them. Personally, this was Shelby's favorite holiday of the year. It was a time when family got together and ate the grand turkey dinner with all the fixings. There was no stress or any worries, they simply gathered for the home cooked meal and enjoyed each other's company. It might have made more sense if Shelby and Todd had alternated years between their respective families but each of their families was small and it was important to spend a few hours with each of them. Of course this meant two full Thanksgiving meals and entirely too much pumpkin pie, but who couldn't eat that delicious meal twice?

This year the family seemed especially mindful of the holiday and from the looks she received, Shelby knew they were truly thankful that she was there to spend it with them. It could have been so different, so devastating if they had had to spend this, her favorite holiday without her. Though Shelby acknowledged that it had been a difficult year, she too thanked the Lord that her life had been spared and that she was now able to spend this special day with her family, Todd and her beautiful children who she loved so dearly. As Shelby stood washing the dinner dishes after dinner, tears blurred her eyes. It was times like these when she realized just how precious and fragile life was.

The weekend after Thanksgiving came with the expectation of excitement for Shelby as she always decorated the house for Christmas at the very same time each year. Some people looked forward to the day after Thanksgiving when they could shop; Shelby looked forward to the weekend after Thanksgiving so she could decorate. Hayleigh and Jonelle didn't understand what was going on but they felt the cheer that was radiating from Shelby. The girls clapped their hands and Hayleigh danced as the sounds of the Christmas music played on the stereo. Shelby sang along with the songs as she pulled string after string of lights and other decorations from the well packed box. Todd had gone to town to get a haircut, but as soon as he returned they were going to go buy a Christmas tree. Although Todd wouldn't be able to set it up until the next day, they could spend this time together as a family picking out the tree and bringing it home. Shelby wanted to make sure that all the lights were working so that when they put them on the tree tomorrow they would sparkle and shine. How excited the girls would be when they saw the tree lit up and the star blinking brightly on the top. It made Shelby smile just to think about it.

After she checked the lights and found them all working, she laid them aside. She would put some of the lights on the windows tonight while Todd was working and save the other strings to put on the tree tomorrow. In the meantime she brought out the cardboard pictures of Santa Claus, his reindeer and the Christmas tree that Hayleigh could help her tape on the windows. This first touch of Christmas started bringing the holiday to life. Hayleigh cheered at seeing all the bright decorations and the exuberance that Shelby seemed to radiate. Jonelle watched Hayleigh intently and began smiling and clapping at the sound of

Hayleigh's excited cheers. Shelby explained each picture to Hayleigh as they taped them to the windows. She couldn't help but laugh when Hayleigh described Santa as ho-ho.

By the time Todd arrived back home, everything but the tree itself and the lights on the windows had been put up. Shelby could see by his expression that all the little touches that she put into making their home festive for the holidays made him happy. Soon they were all on their way to the corner lot near the grocery store where Todd chose a tree that would soon come to life with lights and ornaments. One tree was as beautiful as the other to Shelby. She knew that even the most lopsided and bare branched tree would glow with holiday cheer as soon as lights and tinsel were hung on it. It didn't matter to her what tree they chose, but Todd always wanted a tree that was perfectly shaped. So, Shelby just left the decision of which tree to pick for him to make. Shelby's enjoyment simply came from the times like these when they were together as a family. The purpose or its outcome wasn't what was important to her, just the infrequent and precious time they all had together.

When they got home Todd seemed to be as anxious to get to work on the tree as Shelby was. Even though he wouldn't have time to set it up before he went in to work, he did go to the basement, hauled out his saw and the tree stand and carried them out onto the porch where the tree had been placed. He then proceeded to trim the excess branches away from the base of the tree, cut the trunk so that it would fit into the stand, and put the stand on. By the time he was ready to leave for work the tree stand was on and the tree lay on the porch, glimmering in the cold air, waiting to be brought in and decorated.

Shelby waited patiently until early the next afternoon to wake Todd up. She had made an extra effort to keep the girls quiet so he would be rested and in the right mood to finish setting up the tree in the living room. He wasn't a patient person and Shelby knew from previous years that Todd had to be in just the right mood to deal with that particular chore. He never seemed to be able to get the tree level in the stand and he couldn't keep it from falling over. He would yell and swear until he finally gave up in frustration. Every year he would end up putting a string around it and fasten each end to the wall on either side of the tree to hold it upright. Shelby was prepared for it this time and already had the small nails, hammer and kite string where it could be easily retrieved when needed.

As soon as Todd had had his breakfast and two cups of coffee, he gave in to Shelby's pleading and excitement and began the task of bringing the tree in and setting it up. Shelby kept the girls occupied in Hayleigh's bedroom. Todd was ornery enough when doing this; she didn't want him to trip over a toy or have an excited child hanging on his leg during the process. She also didn't want to chance his dark mood ruining either hers or the girl's excitement, so being in a different room was as much for their benefit as it was for Todd's.

Shelby could hear Todd wrestling with the tree and heard the frustration in his voice. Finally, he yelled angrily. "Shelby, get me the hammer and some string."

Shelby smiled silently and ran to where she had put them. She quickly gathered them and took them in to Todd. She let him mutter and spew as she held the tree up so he could hammer the nails into the wall and securely fasten the tree. With Shelby's assistance, it only took a few minutes to complete the job, and as soon as Shelby was sure she was no longer needed, she went back into Hayleigh's bedroom to check on the girls. They were fine. Jonelle was still on the blanket that Shelby had lain on the floor for her, although she had rolled several times and was in an opposite corner from where she had been when Shelby had left the room. It made Shelby smile, pretty soon she would be would be crawling and pulling herself up on furniture and Shelby wouldn't be able to let her out of her sight. Hayleigh was turning the pages of her book, her Kermit frog laid closely by her side. They were such good children. Shelby felt so blessed very time she looked at them. They both looked up expectantly as Shelby walked into the bedroom and automatically smiled. Shelby walked over and scooped up Jonelle and held her snugly while outstretching her hand to Hayleigh.

"Come on Hayleigh. Daddy put the Christmas tree up. Let's go see it."

Hayleigh jumped right up and ran to grab her mommy's hand and then they all ran together into the living room. Thankfully, the look on Todd's face told Shelby that he wasn't irritated any longer. In fact, with the job now completed, and a gleeful squeal from Hayleigh, Todd's mood had improved immensely. He smiled and spread his arms wide as an invitation for Hayleigh to run into them. He swung her around and carried her over to look at the tree, then put her down and walked over to Shelby and held out his hands, inviting Jonelle into his arms to hug. Shelby's sentimental emotions got the best of her and her eyes welled up with tears. One escaped down her cheek. She quickly wiped it away, only wanting her children to see the glowing smile on her face.

They spent the afternoon decorating the tree and after the last piece of tinsel was placed on it; Todd and Shelby sat on the couch so they could see yet another breathtaking masterpiece they had created, and also to watch the girl's enchanted eyes looking at the colorful blinking lights.

Thus, started the rush of the Christmas season. Before she knew it, it was Christmas Eve and Shelby was at her parent's house with her family enjoying a delicious ham dinner. The feast had been prepared and set on the table along with the holiday china that Shelby's mother kept for this one meal every year. The lace tablecloth that had been Shelby's great grandmother's lay elegantly beneath the gleaming china and steaming food.

After the wonderful meal and desserts of apple and pumpkin pie, everyone sat in the living room around the silver Christmas tree that had been passed down from Shelby's grandmother. Presents were opened and while Shelby played with the girls and their new toys on the floor, Todd and Shelby's father and her brothers went into the kitchen to get a beer. They sat around laughing and talking and eventually Shelby's brothers returned to the living room so they could turn on the TV to watch the previews of the football bowl game that was going to be played on Christmas day.

During a break in the conversation, Shelby's father looked down at the ground then up so that his eyes met Todd's. The smile disappeared from his face and a look of concern came over it.

"How is Shelby doing, Todd? Is she still having as many anxiety attacks?"

Todd took a deep breath then exhaled it just as deeply. He looked down to his hands that were clasped between his knees where his elbows rested. "To tell you the truth, I think they're getting worse. She tries to hide the attacks from me, but I can tell by the look in her eyes that she's scared to death most of the time." Todd had noticed that ever since the daylight hours had shortened, she seemed to be withdrawing into the protective cocoon of the house more and more. He somberly continued. "I've even woken up to find her visibly shaking. Besides holding her, there just doesn't seem to be anything I can do to help her."

"Well, do you think it would help if she lived in another house where maybe she wouldn't be reminded of what happened every day?"

"I've thought about that myself. Shelby keeps telling me that she loves the house we're living in and that it doesn't bother her because she doesn't remember anything. But I think she's afraid it's going to happen again. Besides, without Shelby working, I could never come up with the money for a down payment on a house."

"Well, Shelby's mother and I have been talking about that. This house is paid for and we could easily get an equity loan. You could use it for a down payment on a house here in town. You'd have to make the payments on the loan as well as your mortgage payment, but this way we can be near if she needs someone while you're at work nights."

Todd was overwhelmed by the generosity of his father-in-law's offer and looked into his eyes, the relief and gratitude evident. "You would do that for us?"

"Of course we would. We want to do anything we can to help. So, what do you think?"

"I think that sounds like a great idea. I think Shelby would feel safer knowing you're right around the corner. I can't wait to tell her." Todd's eyes welled up with tears and he thrust his hand out to shake his father-in-laws hand.

So with a hand shake and a pat on the shoulder, Shelby's father-in-law nodded and got up to get another beer. Todd sat there for a few minutes longer, trying to collect his thoughts and emotions. He could not believe that anyone could be so gracious and helpful. He smiled, shook his head and took a deep breath. Then, got up and walked into the living room where Shelby still sat on the floor playing with the girls. He sat on the chair in back of her, reached for her shoulder and rubbed it gently with his hand. When Shelby turned around and smiled warmly at him, his only thought was that this was an absolutely perfect Christmas.

* * *

Chapter Fourteen

Everyone in the family kept their ears and eyes open for properties that were for sale in the small village where Shelby's parents lived. By mid-winter, she and Todd had looked at a few houses, but they were all too expensive. Finally, a house came on the market that was in their price range. Even though it was an older fixer-upper house, it seemed to be solid and it was only a block from her parent's house so they agreed to buy it.

The excitement of the move and the work necessary to make the house into their new home preoccupied Shelby. The fear and panic attacks seemed to subside. Although they didn't go away completely, Shelby found that she was more relaxed and that the attacks were less severe. For that she was grateful, and she hoped that maybe they would finally stop.

Shortly thereafter, the criminal trial for her assailant started. But, as the District Attorney had told her not to attend the proceedings, Shelby was oblivious to what was occurring in the courtroom. She sat in the waiting area of the courtroom for days on end nervously waiting to be called to testify. Finally, it was her turn. She was escorted to the witness stand and soon discovered that the moment she had been anxiously waiting for was profoundly anti-climatic. She gave her quick testimony, that she didn't know or remember what happened, and then she was escorted back out. It wasn't until she was back in the waiting area that she realized that during her short period on the stand, she never even looked at the defendant. Not once had she looked at the man who had attacked her so savagely. She didn't know if it was a conscious decision on her part to avoid putting a face to the brutality of the assault, or whether she had simply been so anxious about the impending questioning, that she just didn't think to look into the eyes of the man that had tried to kill her. Maybe if she would have, she would have at least had a single face to equate with this overwhelming fear she felt.

Finally after days of testimony and presentation of evidence, the verdict was handed down. Not guilty!

When Todd came out of the courtroom and informed her of the final verdict, Shelby was stunned and her mind began swirling with unsettling thoughts. *How could that possibly be? A man had entered her home, viciously beat her, tried to rape her and when he couldn't, he went outside, picked up the shovel that lay next to the back porch, brought it and tried to kill her by chopping her head with it. And he was found not guilty? My God, he had even been found in her bedroom covered with her blood. How could he possibly be found not guilty?*

Shelby grasped Todd's arm for support herself and to try to reel in her confusion and shock. She wanted to ask him how the jury could have possibly come to that verdict, but she saw the fury on his face and bit back the question. She had never seen him look so angry before and she didn't want to say or do anything that would trigger the obvious violence that was building inside him. He didn't comfort her or reassure her. In fact, he didn't say anything at all as they stood outside the courtroom door. His eyes stared off into the distance, his lips were a tight, thin line beneath the dark mustache, and his stance was stiff and unrelenting. It was apparent to Shelby that he was taking the loss in court very personally. As if it were his case on trial, not hers. She had no idea what the anger stemmed from. Whether it was the juror's decision itself, the way the case was presented by the District Attorney and the Public

Defender, or whether it was the fact that they had put their faith in the legal system and it had failed them. Whatever it was, it had brought his anger to a level that Shelby had never seen it rise to before.

Shelby's father turned to her and immediately wrapped his arms around her shoulder to pull her tightly to him. Shelby could hear the sorrow in his voice when he said softly. "Everything is going to be okay Shelby; you don't have anything to worry about."

Shelby's mind raced as she wondered if anything was ever going to be okay again. What if this guy came back again in the middle of the night to finish what he hadn't completed the first time? Todd still worked nights and she was still alone with her daughters. The only thing that wasn't the same was the fact that they now lived in a different house. It wouldn't be hard to find out where they lived as it was just a small village. Oh, how Shelby wished Todd would understand that she needed him with her during the night.

The days that followed the trial were filled with the uncertainty of her safety as well as her daughter's. It was at the forefront of her mind during most of her waking hours. In fact, the hours that she slept became fewer and fewer. Shelby felt that she again had to be on guard to protect her children during the darkness of night while Todd was at work. When she did sleep, it was so light that she would wake at the least little noise that the girls or the house made. Shelby was keenly aware of each squeak the wooden house made, the sound of the branches of the large maple trees gently rubbing against the siding and the rustle of her daughters tossing in their beds. These sounds became engrained in her mind. If there happened to be an unfamiliar noise, one that piqued her inner alarm, her eyes would open wide and she would concentrate every ounce of her attention on that noise until she could figure out what it was and where it came from.

She frequently lay in bed, scared to death. Her heart would beat erratically one minute and race the next. Sometimes, the space between the beats was so long that Shelby was sure her heart had quit beating altogether. Then, inexplicably, her heart would beat so fast and so hard that it seemed as though her heart was convulsing. Shelby could not only hear her heart beat but, as she looked at her chest, she was sure she could literally see it hammering against her ribs. She wanted to scream, but she couldn't. Her chest felt as if someone was sitting on it. She could barely breathe, let alone cry out.

Somewhere deep inside her, she knew she was just having another panic attack, that she wasn't dying and that it would all pass. But, my God, she was scared. If she hadn't been through this time after time, she would have sworn that something was terribly wrong with her. She would fearfully look towards the phone that was on the dresser, willing herself to get up and call for an ambulance as she couldn't protect her children if she died.

She had to concentrate on her breathing, slow it down. *Breathe in through your nose and blow the breath out of your mouth slowly* Shelby told herself. *Good, do it again, the same thing, slowly breathe in through your nose and then blow the breath out. You're going to be fine. See, your fingers aren't tingling any more and your hands aren't shaking. Breathe slowly and relax. There, see? Your heart is slowing down and your chest doesn't feel like its being squeezed. You're all right. You're not having a heart attack. You're not dying. You're okay now.*

Her heartbeat and breathing returned to normal and Shelby curled up in a ball hiding her face in her pillow to muffle her heart wrenching sobs. If Todd were there, he could hold her in his protective arms and she wouldn't be afraid. Shelby fretfully wondered why this was happening almost every day again. She thought she was getting better.

Emotionally and physically drained from another severe panic attack, Shelby eventually dropped off into an exhausted sleep. She slept restlessly until Todd arrived home from work. It wasn't until after he got into bed, until she would feel his body curl into hers that her fear was erased. She could then let down her defenses, and sleep peacefully until the girls woke up, ready to start a new day.

The fear was imprisoning Shelby. She rearranged their furniture so that her living room and dining room were switched. The living room and its attached play area were surrounded on three walls by windows and the front door. In contrast, the dining room, set in the middle of the house, only had the one window. Therefore, Shelby felt more protected and less visible to the outside world in the dining room. Besides, the room was large, almost larger than the living room, and it was void of a dinette set as they couldn't afford to buy one, so it was just utilized as a playroom for the girls. She was able to convince Todd and her family that the switch made perfect sense, and escaped having to explain that she just wanted to stay as far away from the windows as possible.

On top of the increasing amount of fear and anxiety that Shelby was feeling, there was increasing pressure for her to go back to work. The financial pinch Shelby and Todd were feeling was getting tighter and tighter. Whereas they only paid a minimal amount of rent when they were living in Todd's grandfather's house, they now had a mortgage payment and a loan payment for the home equity loan Shelby's parents had obtained for them, as well as all the other bills that came along with home ownership. The half acre yard they now had, necessitated them buying a used riding mower. The property taxes, homeowner's insurance and everything else added strain to Todd's paycheck. It was becoming imperative that Shelby get a full-time job.

And she did. Shelby couldn't help but think how lucky she was. She found a job, doing cost accounting at a downtown business. She was able to walk back and forth from work, so Todd could have the car for his use. And, more importantly, Louise came over to Shelby's each morning, picked the girls up, and took them to her house so that she could baby-sit her granddaughters until Todd woke up and came to pick them up. Shelby was grateful for all the help her parents were giving them. They never hesitated to help in any way they could.

Unfortunately, her increasing emotional problems took their toll on Shelby. She was battling demons that she didn't know how to fight. She wasn't sleeping at all during the night and in situations where she wasn't completely aware of what was going on around her, she became so frightened that she could feel the blood drain from her face as she began to shake. The feeling of dread engulfed her and she would defensively turn around in every direction to make sure there was no one lurking, ready to pounce on her. It didn't matter that the doors were securely locked; she knew that if evil wanted to get to you, the locks couldn't stop it. It took every ounce of strength she had, not to scream. Her fear was so intense. She came close to a nervous breakdown and it affected her concentration at work. She started being inconsistent and made errors in the calculations of the cost of good sold, and after five months, she was let go.

She felt absolutely devastated as she walked home after being fired. *What would Todd say? How would they pay their bills? How could she have let something like this happen, especially when she enjoyed her job and knew she could do the work? Why was she scared all the time?*

Shelby knew she had to do something about the panic attacks that were taking over her life. So she made another appointment with her doctor to see if there was another medication other than Valium that she could take. Although the Valium helped her body relax whenever fear started to take control, her thoughts were still racing in a paranoid state. Her heart would still race as she imagined scenarios of someone lurking in a closet, behind a door, around the corner of the next room, upstairs when she was downstairs, downstairs when she was upstairs, or outside peering in the window. Shelby felt foolish. She felt she had the mindset of a small child fearful of a monster under their bed. But she couldn't control the fear; it was taking over her life.

After a lengthy discussion, Dr Mitchum assured her that he would find another medication that would help alleviate her symptoms. Shelby could only hope and pray that he would find something that would help her get her life back. That was how she felt, like her life was slowly being taken from her.

Shelby made a follow-up appointment and after she arrived at the doctor's office, she sat in the chair of the examination room expectantly waiting for Dr. Mitchum to walk in. When he did, the smile on his face gave Shelby hope. She saw what she thought was a victorious expression on his face. Was it possible? Had he found a medication that would help her? Shelby started to feel exuberant, even before Dr. Mitchum had even said hello. After a careful review of what Shelby had previous told him about how the Valium made her feel, the doctor told Shelby that he looked into the matter further and was sure he had found a medication that would help alleviate the symptoms she described.

She left the office with her prescription of Xanax in her hand and went to the pharmacy to have it filled. The doctor had been adamant when he explained that this wasn't a cure for the fear she had, but if she took the medication at the onset of an attack, it would stop it and she would feel relaxed, both physically and mentally. It worked differently than the body numbing Valium. If the medication worked, he was going to prescribe the lowest dosage available and have her take it once a day, preferably at bedtime. This would hopefully be a preventative means to alleviate the panic attacks all together, or at least, reduce the severity and the number of occurrences. Of course, he also recommended that she see a psychiatrist. Instead of taking the comment personally, she took it as it was meant to be, another outlet of helping her deal with what had happened to her. Maybe with continued therapy sessions, she may get to the point where she might not even need the medication any more.

Could it be possible? Shelby looked at the small bottle of pills in her hand as she sat in the car after leaving the pharmacy. Could this medication stop whatever was going on with her? She was somewhat skeptical, unable to grasp the concept of a tiny pill relieving her from the burden of these episodes that were becoming debilitating. She also looked at the appointment card in her other hand.

Dr. Mitchum hadn't taken the chance that Shelby might forget to follow up with the psychiatrist and had had the receptionist make an appointment for her.

Shelby knew what she was going through was crazy, but she knew she wasn't crazy. Todd was acting as if he had serious doubts about that, and Shelby realized that it was probably impossible for him, or anyone that hadn't experienced a panic attack, to comprehend what it was like. Like Dr. Mitchum, it was going to be a welcome relief to speak with someone who knew what she was experiencing and, who might be able to help her deal with her assault. That appointment was not for a couple weeks yet. In the meantime, she would see how this medication worked. The hope of there being a measure of normalcy in her life again was enough to bring a spontaneous smile to Shelby's face. Maybe, she thought, just maybe I'll return to the person I once was.

After two weeks on the medication, Shelby could clearly see that her life was transforming. Even though she continued to have anxiety attacks, they were nowhere near as intense as before. Instead of feeling like someone was sitting on her chest, suffocating her, and having her heart beat so fast and so hard that she was sure she could visibly see her chest pulse with each quick beat, her heart beat only seemed to flutter in the midst of an attack now. Instead of fearing that there was someone lurking, waiting to get her, she simply felt an annoying uneasiness that made her double check to make sure the doors were locked before she ran the cleaner, took a shower, or went to bed. What a relief this was to Shelby. She didn't really care if she had to spend the rest of her life on this medicine; it had indeed given Shelby her life back. She and the girls spent more time outside and more daylight hours with the blinds open, although Shelby still had to have the blinds pulled as soon as darkness came. And, during the short days of the winter, the blinds were closed quite early. But, she knew that when you walked past a window during the darkness of night, you could see into a house and the occupants couldn't see you outside. Shelby was careful now. She paid attention to things she had never even thought about before. All for the sake of protecting herself and especially her children when Todd wasn't around, a situation that was becoming more and more frequent.

Shelby felt on top of her game again and she soon found a full-time accounting job at Meadow Lane Dairy Products in Johnstown. She loved working with numbers and felt capable and confident again. Her parents were so giving and helpful. Not only did Louise care for her grandchildren, but they also let Shelby use their only vehicle to drive back and forth to work. Shelby would drop the girls off at her mothers, take her father and drop him off where he worked and then went to her own job. Her employers were nice enough to give her a slight adjustment in her work hours so that all of this could be accomplished. At the end of the workday, Shelby's father would catch a ride home with a co-worker or walk home. He never complained and always insisted that it really wasn't any problem at all. Fortunately, a couple months after Shelby started her new job; Todd was offered a position as a deputy for the county. Along with the new position he was assigned a patrol car that he was able to drive back and forth to work. This alleviated his need to drive their personal vehicle every afternoon to work and allowed Shelby to use the car.

Finally, everything seemed to be going smoothly. Although Shelby only saw Todd a couple evenings a week, she had the girls to keep her busy. Todd worked the 6:00 until 2:00 shift. So the only time Shelby got to see him for any amount of time was on Tuesday and Wednesday evening when he had off and on Saturday and Sunday's before he went in to work. The girls were at least able to spend a few hours with him each day, and he did make a point of stopping in to see Shelby at the house whenever he was patrolling in the area. Shelby was ecstatic every time she saw the patrol car pull into the driveway.

After Todd got up in mid-morning, he usually went out for his morning coffee and then would pick the girls up at Louise's. After their afternoon naps, he would play with them until Shelby got home from work. She made it home just in time for him to give her a kiss and rush out the door on his way to work. Shelby thought that by now she should be used to Todd's work schedule, but the fact was, she missed him terribly. She loved him and always enjoyed it when they spent time together. It didn't matter whether they did anything or not. His closeness, his touch, his voice, just his very presence near her made her giddy. She couldn't say whether it was because she was still so in love with him, or whether it was due to the popular saying, that absence makes the heart grow fonder. Whichever the case, she wished they were able to have more time together. Actually, it wouldn't be so bad if Todd would at least tune police work out during the small increments of time that he was able to spend with her. Todd seemed to be obsessed with his job. Everything he did and said seemed to gravitate around it. Nothing else seemed to matter or at least nothing else seemed to be as important as what was going on at the Sheriff department.

It wasn't that they never had any fun together; it was just that those times occurred so seldom. Always in competition with his job, if there was something in particular that Shelby thought would be fun to do, Todd would check his schedule, then think about it carefully and decide whether it was something he was willing to take off work for. Shelby would be so happy whenever he would agree that it sounded like a good idea and would be fun for all of them. Like the time they took the girls to the Ice Capades. Even though the girls were still young and weren't exactly sure what was going on when the show began, the excitement in the auditorium was contagious. All the children in the crowd cheered when the Disney characters skated around the rink. The music made it all become familiar to the girls and they were swept up in the excitement. It was magical for Shelby to watch the girls squeal with glee as they watched not only the characters, but at the lighted wands and glow-in-the-dark rings around the necks of the cheering children.

They also spent long, relaxing days at the zoo. As they Walked through the exhibits, it was so much fun to see the look in Hayleigh's eyes as she recognized the animals she had only seen on the pages of her many books. Afterwards, they would return to the car, get the picnic lunch that Shelby had prepared earlier, and walk to the small park across the street from the entrance of the zoo. Todd would then lay the blanket out on the ground beneath a beautiful maple tree that provided shade. When they got the girls seated, Shelby would pull out a juice box for a very thirsty Hayleigh and made a bottle for Jonelle. As Shelby fed Jonelle, Todd would get the fried chicken; tuna shell salad and two cans of pop from the cooler. Then he'd find the paper plates, plastic spoons and napkins that Shelby had packed in the bag that also had a bag of potato chips in it. They all ate contentedly. The girls, very sleepy from the adventure and their full stomachs, slept peacefully in their car seats during the hour drive back home. Shelby didn't think there could be anything better than days like this, where they didn't have a care in the world and they were all happy and having so much fun together. Of course, that would all end as soon as they got home and Todd rushed to get his uniform on so he could be out the door and off to his other life.

Despite the fact that Shelby somehow felt she and the girls had taken second place to Todd's job, she was very proud of him. He had started his career excitedly but with reserve and apprehension as he didn't have a lot of self-esteem. And now, here he was a member of the Sheriff department who had achieved respect for the outstanding work he did. He had grown confident as a person as well as a police officer. He would hold her in his arms and thank her for her encouragement and support. In some ways, Shelby knew that it was her unconditional love for him that had allowed him to bloom into the person who could walk with his head high and his heart full.

* * *

Chapter Fifteen

Shelby rose and looked at the clock; it was only 5:00 in the morning. What was the hall light doing on? She looked back towards Todd and saw him sleeping soundly next to her. Then she heard the pitter patter of little feet running around in the girls' bedroom. She smiled to herself and climbed out of bed. She ran her hand through her hair that was long and flowing once again and retrieved her housecoat from the back of the bedroom door. As she slipped her arms into it, she walked towards the bedroom that the two young girls shared. Jonelle was still sleeping soundly in her twin size bed with her favorite blanket held tightly in her little hands.

Hayleigh looked up excitedly at her smiling mother from where she sat on the bedroom floor. She had just finished putting on her new sneakers. With overflowing enthusiasm she said, "Mommy, I just couldn't sleep any longer. This is my first day of school!"

Shelby raised her finger to her lips to encourage Hayleigh to be quiet so she wouldn't wake Jonelle. "Shhhh. You'll wake your sister up. I see you're already dressed in the clothes we laid out last night. Why don't we go down and get some breakfast, then I'll braid your hair for you, okay?"

When Shelby held out her hand, Hayleigh ran over and grabbed it tightly. She had a skip in her step as they walked back down the hallway and down the stairs. Knowing how long Hayleigh had to wait before it was time to go to school; Shelby invited her to help prepare french toast and scrambled eggs. It was Hayleigh's favorite breakfast. Normally, it was so hectic in the morning; the girls would have a quick bowl of cereal, while Shelby got ready for work. It was nice for them to have this opportunity to slow down and enjoy a relaxing breakfast together.

She had already decided to go in to work a little later than usual so that she could see Hayleigh get on the bus for the first time. Shelby handed Hayleigh her apple juice and watched as her little girl fidgeted and pushed her breakfast around on her plate between bites. Shelby wanted to tell her not to play with her food, but she knew how excited Hayleigh was about starting school. She had been inquisitive since she was a toddler. She could always be found in the midst of a pile of her favorite books and loved to have stories read to her. She had always had the ability to learn everything quickly. How to tie her shoes, how to say her ABC's, how to count, and how to write her name. For the last month, she had been eagerly anticipating the start of the school year and rejoiced as she crossed off the dates on the calendar marking the days remaining before the first day of school.

After eating all that she could reasonably be expected to eat, Shelby leaned against the door in the bathroom and watched as Hayleigh washed her hands and face, then brush her teeth. When she was all done, Shelby grasped Hayleigh's hand and they walked into the living room. Shelby sat on the couch and smiled as Hayleigh automatically plopped down on the floor between her mother's feet. Her back faced Shelby, ready to have her mom brush her long light brown hair and began braiding it. Shelby did this every day, with both girls. She usually braided their hair into two pigtails, but today Hayleigh just wanted it pulled back into one long braid. She normally wasn't too concerned with what her mom did with her hair but, today was special. The previous evening, she had taken a long time trying to decide which of her new outfits she wanted to wear on her first day of school. This was a very important day to her and Shelby was more than happy to treat it as the special occasion that it was.

Shelby got dressed and then read several stories to Hayleigh. At 7:00, Shelby finally allowed the little girl to go wake her daddy up so he could see her get on the bus. Hayleigh ran right up the stairs and headed straight for Todd's bed at full speed. When he had left for work the evening before, Todd had held Hayleigh tightly and told her to promise to wake him up so he could watch her get on the big yellow school bus. Hayleigh had bobbed her head up and down and promised she would. Then she had thrown her arms around her daddy's neck and hugged him tightly.

Shelby sighed as her exuberant daughter disappeared up the stairs. Hayleigh had reminded Shelby several times throughout the early hours of the morning that she just had to go wake her daddy up. Shelby held her off as long as she could. She knew that Todd had gotten in later than usual from work and had only been sleeping for a few hours, so she wanted to make sure he was able to sleep as long as possible before Hayleigh woke him up. Shelby stood at the bottom of the stairs listening to her daughter's excited voice.

"Daddy. Daddy. Wake up. The bus is going to come get me for my first day of school."

Shelby relaxed when she heard Todd's sleepy response. He sounded tired, but good natured as he jokingly asked her if she was sure she had the right day. Soon Hayleigh appeared dragging her daddy by the hand down the stairs into the kitchen and then over to the calendar where that days date was circled in bright red crayon.

"See, it is today," she said emphatically.

"Yep, I guess you're right. If your mommy will make me a cup of coffee, I'll go get dressed so I can go out with you, okay?" Todd looked at Shelby and smiled as he stood in his pajama bottoms. Shelby had walked over to the kitchen entryway after she was assured Todd was awake and she leaned against the doorframe watching him as he walked hand in hand down the stairs with Hayleigh. His hair was disheveled, his eyes were sleepy and the new day's growth of whiskers on his chin was dark and scruffy looking. He was bare-chested as he only wore pajama bottoms to bed. Shelby momentarily forgot about the excitement of the morning as her body heated up just looking at her husband. He had a broad chest, muscular arms, a flat toned stomach and his pajama bottoms hung low on his narrow hips. She was thunderstruck at the realization that she was still filled with desire whenever she was near him or looked at him as she did now.

She smiled back and nodded as she walked over to give him a kiss good morning. She couldn't help but think how wonderful it would be if they had more mornings together like this.

While Todd dressed, Jonelle woke up. So when the big yellow bus rounded the corner on its way to pick up Hayleigh, Todd held Jonelle in one arm and had his other arm encircling Shelby's waist as they stood on the porch watching. When the bus arrived, Shelby felt a strong desire to go and pull her baby back into her arms and tell the bus to go ahead without her. It was very hard for Shelby to let her go. As the tears welled up in her eyes, she watched as Hayleigh turned around quickly with a rushed wave goodbye and eagerly climbed the tall steps of the school bus. As the bus took off, Jonelle waved feverishly and Shelby raised her hand to wave goodbye to her beloved daughter. How could she be sad, when Hayleigh was being such a big girl and rejoicing at this new step in her life? Shelby swallowed her tears, smiled widely and waved at their little girl who was looking out the window with a huge smile on her face.

The following weeks seemed to fly by as usual and as Shelby was getting the girls ready to go out Trick or Treating for Halloween, it suddenly dawned on her that she hadn't had her period at all in October. Oh my God, she thought. I haven't had a period since right after Hayleigh started school at the beginning of September. She was always very regular, but she couldn't be pregnant. She felt fine, no morning sickness at all like she had with both the girls, and she had used birth control religiously, so no she couldn't be.

She was worried though. If she were pregnant, she wouldn't be able to take her medicine if she had a panic attack as it might harm the baby. She had been able to back off from taking it every night and was again only using it when she had a full-blown panic attack, which wasn't very often. In fact, she hadn't felt the need to take the medicine in months, so at least she didn't have to worry whether she had taken any, IF she was pregnant.

She also worried what Todd would say. Then she realized she didn't even know if there was a reason to worry. Fortunately, Todd was working like he always did on Halloween, and he wouldn't notice her nervousness. She decided to call her obstetrician first thing in the morning to make an appointment to see what was going on.

Two days later, while Shelby was on her lunch break, she went to the doctor's office and found out that she was indeed pregnant. She was due right before Hayleigh got done with the school year. Even though this child wasn't planned like the other two had been, Shelby was just as happy. She had always wanted three children, and now, with Hayleigh in school and Jonelle an independent three and a half year old, Shelby was ready for another baby. She loved children, especially babies and couldn't wait to hold this one in her arms.

That afternoon when she got home from work, Todd was there. It was his day off and he was busy playing with the girls. Shelby always wistfully hoped to find that Todd would have a simple dinner prepared when she arrived home from work. At least once in a while. But she laughed at herself for being so silly, as Todd had stated more than once that cooking wasn't part of his job description. Shelby couldn't find it in her to get upset with Todd though. The girls were so happy to be able to spend this time in the afternoon with him. Shelby always found it easy to overlook this and any of his other shortcomings. After giving each of the girls a loving hug and kiss, she bent over to kiss Todd, who was sitting on the floor with a wooden puzzle.

"Hi," Shelby said warmly as she smiled at Todd and ran her fingers through his mussed up hair. "Looks, like you're having fun here. Are you getting hungry?

"We're having all sorts of fun," Todd said sarcastically with a smile on his face. "I think I've put this puzzle together at least 20 times." As he got up off the floor, he continued. "We all had peanut butter and jelly sandwiches when Hayleigh got home from school so we're not starved. What's for dinner anyway?" he asked.

"I have some pork chops thawed out. Does that sound alright?" she asked, trying hard not to think about the fact that he'd been home all day and could have tossed them in the oven himself.

"Sure, that sounds good," Todd said oblivious to Shelby's silent thoughts. "You seem awful cheerful tonight, something special happen at work today?"

"Hey, I'm always happy, especially when you're here with us," Shelby said teasingly. "But I did get some good news today."

"What, are you getting a big raise or something?" Todd said excitedly.

"No, nothing like that." Shelby said, still smiling, as she turned and opened the refrigerator door to get out the pork chops.

"Wait, a minute. You're acting like the cat that ate the canary again. You're not..." Todd asked hesitantly.

Shelby turned around and looked at him. She could swear she physically saw the blood drain out of his face as he stood there with his mouth dropping open. "Yes, I am. Oh, Todd," Shelby said enthusiastically. "I don't know how it happened. I mean, you know I always use birth control. But, somehow I got pregnant anyway. We're going to have another baby in June."

"Oh God Shelb, how are we going to manage with three kids?" Todd said as he sat down heavily into the kitchen chair.

"I don't know, but we'll figure it out, don't worry," Shelby said as she went over and put her hand around his shoulder, and then kissed the top of his head. "I was a little shocked at first too, but now, I couldn't be happier. I love you Todd and one way or the other, everything will work out fine."

Todd was still shell-shocked, but apparently wasn't able to resist the gentleness and cheer in Shelby's voice. He wrapped his arm around her waist and pulled her closer to him so that his face nuzzled in her breast. "Yeah, everything will work out just fine. By the way, how do you feel?"

Although Shelby could have stayed wrapped in Todd's arms all evening, she knew she had to get dinner going, so she slowly pulled away from him. She kissed him as he looked up towards her, and then she walked over to the counter. "It's actually amazing. I feel great. I haven't had a bit of morning sickness; I guess that's why it never hit me that I might be pregnant."

"You're going to be able to keep working for a while then?" Todd said nervously, obviously thinking about their financial situation.

"Yeah, though I've heard that they're talking of closing our branch of the plant down. If they do, I'll be getting laid off anyway. But, I'll work as long as I can or as long as I have a job to go to."

Todd nodded his head, seemingly happy that he wouldn't have to worry about how they were going to pay their bills. For the time being anyway.

Finding out that they were going to have a third child made Todd tighten the money belt even further. As they already had a wood stove, they decided to go in halves with Shelby's parents and buy a load of logs that they could cut and use for heat during the swiftly approaching winter. As soon as the logs were delivered to Shelby's parent's house, Todd spent every available minute he had over there cutting them up on the wood splitter they had rented. After the logs were split, Todd borrowed his brother-in-laws truck and brought half of the wood home and piled it in their garage.

They weren't sure how much wood they would go through during the winter, but Todd had a pretty substantial supply stacked up. They could only hope that it would be enough.

All too soon the cold winter wind began to blow and the warm, comforting heat of the wood stove felt good. It was definitely a different heat than the hot water baseboard heating that they were used to. The upstairs was noticeably cooler and so was the bathroom that was towards the back of the house but, the downstairs living room, dining room and kitchen were almost hot. As they worked different shifts, they were able to keep the fire going constantly and the house was always toasty.

At the end of the year, Shelby received her notification that the plant site where she worked was indeed shutting down. Although she would be out of work in a few weeks, she would be able to receive unemployment benefits. She would also be able to spend some quality time with Jonelle before the baby arrived. Where Hayleigh had always been inquisitive and independent, Jonelle was shy and followed in her mother's footsteps wherever she went. Shelby could tell that Jonelle loved having her mommy back home again and the little girl never seemed to get her fill of cuddling on Shelby's lap. Jonelle had missed Hayleigh since she had started school and was understandably a little lonely without her sister there for her to play with all the time.

During late spring, when Shelby was almost seven months along, Todd announced to her that he had been talking to his friend Mark, who was now living in Florida, and that Mark had asked Todd to come down to visit him and his new wife. Todd said that Mark's uncle, who also lived down there, had said that there were some security jobs available at a large turbine engine manufacturing plant. Mark's aunt and uncle were also moving into a new house they had built which would leave their current house available to rent if Todd was offered a job at the plant and decided to move down there.

"Todd, when did you decide that you wanted to move to Florida and get a new job?" Shelby said in an alarmed voice.

"I didn't," Todd said defensively. "I was just talking to Mark last night and one thing led to another and I thought maybe it would be a good opportunity to check it out. That's all. Plus," he said, his eyes flicking away briefly before returning to Shelby. "I haven't seen Mark in a while and it would be nice to go visit him."

"Just you?" Shelby asked, astonished by what she was hearing. "You weren't thinking of taking the girls and me with you?"

"Aw, Shelb. You're pretty far along and you shouldn't be so far from home in case something happens. And besides," Todd quickly added. "Hayleigh has school; you wouldn't want her to miss anything."

"Todd, that's ridiculous," Shelby said emphatically. "Hayleigh is doing great in school; it wouldn't hurt her at all to miss a few days. And, I'm not due for two months, I'll be just fine. In fact, it would probably be good for all of us to get some sun and fresh air."

"Yeah, I know it would be great for all of us to get away. It would make a nice vacation. But, Mark only has a one bedroom apartment and I'd be sleeping on the couch if I went. Where would we all sleep?"

"I didn't think about that," Shelby exhaled with disappointment. "You really want to go down and visit by yourself don't you?"

"Would you mind?" Todd said humbly. "I'll only go down for a few days; check things out and come back."

Shelby felt abandoned, but what could she say? *No, you can't go without us. No, you can't check into a new job and home for us to relocate to. No, you can't go visit your good friend.* "I guess so, but don't make any final decision about the job until we get a chance to talk about it, okay?"

"Okay, I'll just go down and check things out," he promised. "Maybe it's nothing I would be interested in anyway. Thanks Shelby," Todd said as he pulled her into his arms and held her tightly. "I love you."

"I love you too," she said as she melted in his gentle but strong embrace.

Todd made all the arrangements to go on his trip, even as far as checking with Bud and Bridget to see if they would drive Shelby to the airport to pick him up when he arrived back from his trip. Shelby was not very confident when it came to city driving and not only would she have to drive through the city to get to the international airport, but she had to drive on the thruway to get there. Shelby got nervous just riding in that traffic; he couldn't see her driving in it.

Shelby thought the idea about riding with Bud and Bridget sounded great. She would leave the girls with Louise and then she could spend some time visiting with Bridget which she hadn't had much of a chance to do lately. With Shelby working full time during the day, they didn't seem to have the opportunity to get together and visit any more. Spending the day together would give them that chance to catch up with one another.

Todd had a co-worker of his take him to the airport one cool spring morning. Shelby was still a little sad that he hadn't worked it out so that she and the girls could go on the trip too but, she reminded herself that he would only be gone a few days. Maybe next time.

Todd had only been gone a day when some very cold weather returned to the area and Shelby discovered they had run out of wood. Shelby wished Todd had checked to see how much wood was left before he took off but, his head must have been in the clouds. He had been so excited about his upcoming trip that he completely forgot about the wood pile.

Shelby just took it in stride and loaded the girls into the car. She went over to her parent's house and visited for a few minutes with Louise, and then she asked her father if she could use some of their wood until Todd got back and figured out what he wanted to do.

"Of course you can," her father said. "Let me get my boots on and I'll put some in the trunk."

"Dad, I can do it, I just wanted to make sure it was all right before I stole some of your wood," Shelby said, smiling at her father.

"Don't be ridiculous," her father said, his voice low and his words clipped short to suppress his growing anger towards his son-in-law. "You're eight months pregnant; you don't need to be out there heaving chunks of wood."

"No, I shouldn't have to," Shelby said as she looked downward in embarrassment. "I would have thought that Todd had made sure we had enough before leaving," her voice disheartened.

"I'll tell you what," her dad said kindly. "I'll load a little in the trunk for you, but then I want you to just turn the furnace on until Todd gets back. You understand?"

"I wish I had thought of that," Shelby said smiling brightly at the simple solution. "Money's been a little tight since I was laid off, but it certainly won't hurt to heat the house for a couple days, and Todd will be back on Sunday."

With that settled, Shelby went home with enough wood to get them through the night. Her father had promised he'd be over first thing in the morning to make sure the pilot light was lit and that everything was safe to start the furnace back up.

Sunday came and Shelby took the girls over to Louise's, then went back home to wait for Bud and Bridget to come get her. After they did, they spent a wonderful afternoon together. As they had some time to spare, they went to an old friend of Bridget's who lived in the area and they also stopped at Bridget's aunt's house. Then after picking Todd up at the airport, they all went out for a quick dinner before driving back home.

As Todd told them all about his trip it sounded to Shelby as though Todd had a really good time. He brought back pictures of the house that Mark's aunt and uncle would have available to rent and pictures of Todd and Mark scuba diving. There was also a disturbingly intimate picture of Todd and Mark's wife. They were sitting quite close to each other, dressed in their swimsuits. Shelby was uneasy about it, but she decided that since Mark was probably the one taking the picture, he had made them move close together.

Todd said that he had indeed had an interview at the engine plant and that it went very well. He said the house they could rent was nice and even had an orange tree in the back yard. But, he said. "While I was driving, I heard a news report that a young child had been kidnapped and murdered." He paused and his face took on a serious look. "Shelb, Florida is nice but there is no feeling of community there. People move there from all over and you don't know what kind of lives they led before they moved there. We might have a serial murderer right in our neighborhood.

We don't have to worry about that here. Everybody knows everybody else and if someone is trouble, you hear about it. I think it would be much safer if we just stayed and raised our kids here."

Since Shelby had never even considered moving, it wasn't any big disappointment when Todd made the solemn proclamation that they should stay where they were instead of moving to Florida. But, she nodded in agreement and then asked.

"What was Mark's wife like? Was she nice?"

"She's quite a partier and I'll tell you what, that marriage is never going to last."

"Why do you say that Todd. They only just got married."

"I just have a feeling, that's all."

Shelby shrugged her shoulders, deciding not to dwell on it. Then she told him about running out of wood and having to turn on the furnace.

"God, I'm sorry, Shelb, he said looking stricken. "I thought about going over to your dad's and picking up some wood for you, but I then I got called in to work because of that burglary and I just forgot all about it. We shouldn't have too much really cold weather left anyway, it's almost May, I'll just get the wood pile cleaned up and clean the stove out and we'll keep using the furnace."

That was fine with Shelby. It would be one less things they had to think about.

A few weeks later, Todd stopped in to see Shelby and the girls while he was patrolling in their area of the county. After hugging and kissing each of the girls that had come to the door squealing "daddy, daddy," he went to Shelby and hugged her tenderly.

"I can hardly get my arms around you," he noted with amusement. "You look like you're about ready to pop."

"I feel like I'm ready to pop," Shelby laughingly agreed. "But I still feel pretty good. I'm lucky this will be over with before it starts getting hot and muggy outside."

"It won't be long now, will it?"

"A couple more weeks is all. The doctor thinks we're going to have another girl, but I've felt so differently during this pregnancy that I think it's going to be a boy," Shelby said as she walked over to the counter to get the glass of water she had set there moments before.

"Well, I've had him named three times now. I hope I don't have to change it to another girl's name," he said as he laughed.

Shelby winced slightly.

"Not really Shelb," he added quickly. "It would be nice to have a boy, but I don't really care. Our girls are kind of nice."

"They are pretty great aren't they?" Shelby agreed lovingly.

"Yes they are," he said as he walked over to where Shelby now stood and pulled her back into his arms. "Hey, I actually stopped by to tell you something," Todd said with a quick laugh.

Shelby was only half listening as she felt light-headed like she always did when Todd held her in his arms. "Yeah, what's that?" she asked sleepily, nuzzling into him, seeking comfort.

Todd cleared his throat and laughed half-heartedly again. "There's a rumor going around town and I thought I'd better tell you before you or your parents hear it," he said nervously.

"What is it, Todd?" Shelby asked quietly. For some reason her heart started to beat fast and she had a sudden feeling of dread.

"Shelb, I don't know who started it, but there's a rumor going around that I left you and moved to Florida." Then he repeated it, as if he was really hearing it for the first time. "That I left you, eight months pregnant, and my two precious little girls and took off for Florida."

"Todd, that's crazy," Shelby laughed, but she noticed the sound of her laugh was brittle in her ears and echoed darkly down her spine. "Why would anyone think something like that, let alone say it?"

Todd exhaled gratefully and then hung his head. "I know it's crazy. I don't know why anyone would say something like that. It's stupid and it isn't true, but I wanted you to know that's what is being said so it doesn't surprise you if you hear it okay?"

Having had a moment to think about what Todd had just told her, Shelby swallowed down the painful lump in her throat and asked. "Todd, were you thinking about leaving us?"

"No. God no, Shelb," Todd almost yelled the words. "It's just a stupid rumor that someone started. Please don't think that I would do anything like that ever Shelb, because I wouldn't."

Shelby could see that Todd was visibly shaken after telling her this, and she turned into his arms, only wanting to be assured that everything was going to be all right.

Shelby never heard any remarks or rumors of that kind and neither did her parents. So, why had Todd told her this? *Did someone threaten to tell her something that he didn't want her to know? Was it all a story or was there a grain of truth to it? Was Todd actually thinking of leaving her?*

Was he so unhappy with his marriage, that he would consider leaving her and the three children? How could that be? He's never complained. We've never even fought. He's hardly ever even home, and when he is, he's lavished with love from her and the girls.

Shelby tried to forget what Todd had told her and busied herself with the preparations for the new baby that would soon arrive.

* * *

Chapter Sixteen

Shelby woke with a start. Her body jerked awake, although her mind was sluggish, caught in thoughts of anticipation for the new baby, love for her girls, and anxiety about her marriage. Disorientated, she lifted her head and surveyed her surroundings, struggling against the confusion that swirled through her mind. The sight of her ever loyal beagle brought the chaos to a halt. He was curled comfortably next to her sleeping soundly. As she pet Charlie's soft, silky fur, Shelby sighed deeply. She realized that she had been in a deep sleep and that what she had just relived was her own personal nightmare. She leaned her head back again as the unsettling memories began to rush vividly into the forefront of her mind.

Was all of this happening because she had grown so much stronger and was finally allowing all of the painful memories that she had locked up so tightly to start seeping through into her conscious thoughts? Maybe this is what she needed to finally be relieved of the deep and sorrowful pain she had experienced while mourning the loss of her marriage and the love of her life. Maybe she was finally realizing that shutting down all those painful memories had also shut down too many good years of her life.

Shelby suddenly realized that she would have to continue to allow those memories to resurface so that she could deal with what happened and learn the lessons that life was teaching her.

Although taking off her rose colored glasses would force her to see things as they were instead of how she wanted them to be, she knew that facing the reality of those memories was just another step she needed to take in healing her heart and soul.

Shelby shook her head and found it hard to believe that before awakening moments ago, she had no memory or recollection of any of those fateful incidents of infidelity by her former husband. She clearly remembered them now; along with the intense heartbreak she felt when something in her gut had told her there was something inappropriate going on. It was as though her mind had blocked these memories, just as a woman blocks the memory of the intense pain she experiences during childbirth. It's one of those natural defenses we're all equipped with to help us survive extreme physical and emotional pain.

Shelby lifted her head from the back of the couch, but kept her eyes closed a moment longer. Even though she had long ago forgiven Todd for the heartache he caused her, she realized that she wouldn't be able to move forward with her life or ever allow her heart to love again unless she allowed these memories to flow freely. She now had to deal with the truth that she hadn't allowed herself to think about during the time she was filled with fear and uncertainty.

Shelby decided that now was as good a time as any. But she needed a few extra moments to summon up the courage she knew she would need to be able to open up that floodgate of agonizing memories that she had pushed deep into her subconscious. She got up slowly and walked to the kitchen to fix a large cup of tea. As the water was heating up, she looked lovingly at Charlie where he lay on the couch. He had popped his head up to see what she was doing. She walked to the front door and said. "Do you want to go out to pee?" The dog quickly jumped off the couch, wagging his tail wildly and trotted to the door excitedly. Shelby hooked him to the run that was on her front patio and watched as he went into the grass. She closed the door and went back into the kitchen to finish making her tea. After dipping the bag repeatedly into the cup of boiling water, she took it out and placed it in her spoon to squeeze out the last remaining droplets of tea. She pulled a package of Equal out of the pantry and put the whole packet in the cup. She had always needed to chase away the bitterness of tea and coffee with a lot of sugar. She then went to the refrigerator and pulled the half gallon container of milk from the door and poured just enough in her cup of tea to change its color. After replacing the milk, Shelby tore off a paper towel and carried it along with the tea back into the living room. She folded the paper towel in half and then in half again. She sat the small square and her cup on the end table next to where she had been sitting. She went to the door and let Charlie back inside and then they both walked back over to the couch. Shelby sat down and quickly curled her feet back up to the side again so the dog could cuddle back into his favorite spot.

Shelby sipped her tea. It tasted so good and the heat of the cup in her hands felt soothing. That was something she sorely needed to give her the strength to allow more memories to resurface.

Shelby now understood that Todd's continuous absence from home contributed to her inability to see that his heart wasn't in the marriage. Could it be possible that the entire marriage, right from the time they said "I do" was a fallacy? Probably, she thought to herself. She had been blinded by her love for Todd, and even though she was sure that some small portion of his heart had belonged to her, she was sure she had romanticized everything else. Todd's ability to say the right things at the right time, and his knowledge that holding her in his arms made her heart melt, made her see things askew of how they actually were. She had viewed her marriage through the rose colored glasses that she wore to hide the fact that Todd was using and abusing her desire to make him happy and fulfilled.

As Shelby forced herself to remember, she realized that the first time she actually thought she might have something to worry about was when their son James was about three years old.

After taking another sip of tea, Shelby sat her cup on the paper towel, leaned her head back and closed her eyes once more. She was ready to face the rest of it now.

* * *

Todd had found a German shepherd puppy that needed a home. It was a welcome addition to the family. It got along well with the children and Shelby felt more secure in the knowledge that with the dog there, their home would be safer during the nighttime when Todd was working. When the puppy was about a year old Todd, feeling drawn to the K-9 division of the department, decided to start obedience training with the dog. The dog progressed rapidly and soon obeyed all of the basic commands that Todd asked of it. There was a problem with this though. The dog only obeyed Todd. He had trained it specifically to obey him and only him. Shelby wasn't permitted to give the dog commands because Todd insisted that it would confuse the animal. Shelby had to keep the dog tied outside at his doghouse most of the time because the large dog became hard for her to control and it scared her to think what might happen when the neighborhood children came to play.

In addition to restricting Shelby from giving the dog even simple commands, Todd adamantly insisted that he needed to train the dog alone after he completed his work shift in the middle of the night. After he arrived home from work, he would retrieve the dog and immediately take him for a walk in the darkness of the night.

As Shelby still automatically woke when Todd arrived home, she would lie there fitfully until he returned from the walk. Sometimes he would return in a short period of time, but usually it was an hour or longer before he returned. When she questioned the need for these late night walks, Todd initially became defensive and then tried to reason with Shelby, explaining that it was the only time of the day he was able to spend alone with the shepherd. He also told her that he was usually so keyed up after work, that the walk helped settle him down. If Shelby had remaining feelings of uneasiness or wasn't entirely convinced with the explanation, Todd would hit on her weak spot, her insecurity.

He would make her feel that she was being unreasonably suspicious and that just because she had all these crazy thoughts going through her head about what he might be doing, she shouldn't try and deprive him of doing what he enjoyed. Embarrassed by what she thought was probably the truth, his comments would do the job and Shelby would be ashamed that she could even allow herself to question his actions.

Eventually as Shelby had dreaded, the dog cornered one of the neighborhood children against a wall and although it didn't hurt the child, she had been scared to death. After this episode occurred, they were forced to find a new home for the dog. Todd was disappointed about that and frequently mentioned how much he missed the dog and their nightly walks. But, Shelby was happy that she once again felt secure and safe with his protective presence in bed with her.

* * *

Shelby was becoming increasingly aware that even all those years ago, Todd wasn't the man she saw him as. Where Todd once gave the pretense of being content, he had turned constantly restless. Where once he was passionate and intimate, he had turned reserved and distant. Where once he was confident yet humble, he had turned cocky and self-centered. Where once he held her at his side with pride and joy, he started keeping her at arms length as if he were embarrassed by her.

* * *

My God, Shelby shuttered. *Why did I allow him to make me feel as if the small amount of attention he gave me was all I deserved? That I was lucky he even stayed with me after I was disfigured and emotionally damaged. Why didn't he just tell me how unhappy he was and that we were in trouble? We could have gone to counseling. We could have dug ourselves out of the hole we were in, instead of digging it deeper and deeper. Maybe even that wouldn't have made any difference. Maybe he just changed his mind. Maybe I wasn't what he needed anymore. Or, maybe he had pretended to be able to handle what had happened to me and just couldn't pretend any longer.*

Whatever they could or should have done differently was beside the point. At the time, Shelby only knew that she believed wholeheartedly in the power of love. She believed that the Lord had brought them together and had made them one when they had married. She believed that they were meant to be together, as man and wife and as parents of the wonderful children they had been blessed with. She felt if she loved him with all her heart, Todd would eventually start returning that love again. Never ever, even in her lowest periods, did she ever think that Todd wouldn't be by her side forever. So no matter what she had to deal with, she hung in there, put her ever present troubles to the way side and concentrated all her attention on her beloved children.

* * *

They had been married nine years when they received invitations to their ten year high school reunion. They had graduated from different schools, but in the same year. Shelby was so excited about going. She hadn't kept in close contact with any of her classmates through the years and was interested in what they were all doing now. But, Todd nonchalantly dropped a bombshell on Shelby's excitement and anticipation of attending.

"I've read that it's better to attend your class reunion by yourself instead of taking your spouse with you. That way, you can relax and spend as much time as you want talking about old times. I think it sounds like a great idea. You go ahead and go to your reunion by yourself and I'll go to mine by myself."

Shelby remembered feeling as if her feet had been knocked out from beneath her. Todd's work schedule gave them little opportunity to go to many social engagements, especially where they could dance, and here he was, taking a Saturday night off, and he didn't even want her to go with him. What could she say? He wasn't asking her opinion about the idea; he was declaring what was going to happen and how it was going to be. No questions were to be asked, no comments were to be made and no argument about the arrangement would matter. His decision was final.

* * *

What would have happened if I had just put my foot down and told him he damn well better take me? Shelby thought to herself. If I had asserted myself, expressed my hurt and anger, my complete outrage at his lack of kindness and respect, would it have made a difference?

* * *

Not only had Shelby been disheartened that Todd didn't want her by his side, she was also admittedly quite uneasy about the fact that Todd's high school sweetheart, the girl he was going steady with before they met, would probably be at his reunion also. Yes, it did bother her; yes she was jealous of a girl who held his heart before she did. There was a history there and with the distance Todd had put between himself and Shelby, she couldn't help but worry whether he would return to her arms.

As he pulled out of the driveway the evening of his reunion, tears streamed down Shelby's face as she watched him out the window of their front door. He didn't look back, he didn't hesitate, he just sped away.

Todd returned in the early hours of the following morning with a half empty bottle of champagne he had won for being married the longest. He was actually laughing as he told Shelby this.

* * *

Shelby shook her head at this unsettling memory. To think that she lived like that; her thoughts and feelings being considered insignificant, and her opinion being ignored as if it didn't matter. Being repeatedly told how stupid and crazy she was for being jealous and insecure whenever he wanted to talk to another woman. The worst part of it, was that outwardly he made it appear to everyone else that they were the all-American couple and family.

During the last three years of their marriage it took everything inside of her to maintain any sense of stability in her everyday life and in the lives of her children. Todd would come home from work, change his clothes, and then walk back out the door without any explanation as to where he was going or when he'd be back. Whenever he was home and they were out of hearing range of the kids, he belittled her and made her feel undeserving of his attention and even his presence.

Shelby began building a wall around herself to protect her from the harsh words and degrading treatment she received. She had to; she didn't want her children to be affected by whatever their problems were. It was important to her that they be raised in a loving and stable environment. She felt that if they had a strong support system, then they would have the strength they needed to be able to face life and its obstacles head-on. She wanted to do everything she could to ensure they were confident in themselves and their abilities. She wanted them to have self-confidence and be independent so that they could stand on their own two feet and succeed in whatever they wanted to do. Most importantly, she wanted them to know what unconditional love was. Shelby felt it, gave it freely to them, and wanted her children to understand how important it was to treat others that way. She couldn't allow them to see how the father that they loved really treated her. She wanted her children to think of him with love and respect.

Though Shelby knew how disillusioned she had been, she could also see how hard she had fought to keep their marriage together and from completely falling apart. She even started thinking that maybe she was acting unreasonably. *Maybe after years of marriage, who was she to think Todd would want to hold her hand lovingly when they walked? Who was she to think that she, who was shy and introverted, could continue to hold his interest? Who was she; a 'plain Jane' to think that she could now compete with so many of the women who swarmed around Todd when he had his uniform on? And besides, even though Todd acted indifferent to her, he had never said anything to indicate that he was unhappy in the marriage and he never expressed that he thought they were having troubles, so maybe this was just what happened between two people that had been together almost twenty years*

* * *

As Shelby began to think about those last years of her marriage, the demeaning and heartbreaking treatment she received from Todd, and the emptiness and despair she felt, she quickly jumped up from the couch and began to nervously pace the room. She wished she still smoked cigarettes. Her hands were shaking. The fact that she could still be shaken by the memory of the verbal and psychological abuse he subjected her too and the unsettling knowledge that she had permitted it to occur at all, let alone for so long, spoke loudly for the confused and desperate state of mind she had been in.

Shelby took several deep breathes and calmed herself. She shook her head slowly, feeling the shame she had felt at that time and also the shame she now felt about allowing a man treat her so inhumanely.

Charlie picked his head up and cocked it sideways, sensing that something unsettling was going on with Shelby. He jumped down off the couch and walked over to her, his tail wagging and his sad eyes looking up at her with concern. Shelby suddenly felt as if the arms of a guardian angel were enveloping her. She felt uplifted, like she had received a new wave of strength, love and support. She kneeled down, hugged her dog tightly and let the smile return to her lips. Shelby remembered the day that Hayleigh had unexpectedly appeared at the door with a smile on her face and the adorable puppy in her arms. Shelby didn't know it at the time, but it had been born on the very day her suspicions of Todd's infidelity had been confirmed. She had discovered that months later, when she was sorting through her files and found his papers. His date of birth all but blazed off the registration form. Tears filled her eyes as she wondered whether the Lord had brought him into her life. He found his way into her home and had been her constant companion and unending source of unconditional love since then.

Her composure back in tact, Shelby knew that it would be much easier for her if she just forget about this quest of hers to bring the reality of her marriage into focus. She tried to tell herself that it wasn't as important as she had originally thought it was. That maybe opening old wounds wasn't the best idea in the world. Even though she was stronger now, maybe it would be better all the way around if she just left things as they were. After all, what good was it going to do to analyze her mistakes and the pain of her past?

Shelby knew the answer to that question. She knew that she couldn't go on with her life without the fear that she would allow the same mistakes to happen again if she didn't face what happened and deal with it head on. Besides, as it was, she was blocking out large portions of her memory, of her past, so that she could avoid reliving the anguish and heartbreak that she had lived with. In the process of blocking out the painful memories, Shelby had realized that she had also blocked out the wonderful years of raising her beloved children. They were her pride and her complete joy. She knew that being a mother of these three children was a blessing bestowed upon her. For her to now be unable to remember the moments they shared together, simply because she didn't want to relive and face the painful portion of that time of her life, was something she no longer found acceptable. She deserved to bask in the glory and happiness of those memories and her children deserved more than a blank stare from her when talking about a particular event. So this was important and more than that, it was absolutely necessary.

Shelby walked to the cupboard and pulled out a package of dog treats. Charlie cheerfully sat up on his hind legs in anticipation of receiving his favorite snack. After giving it to him, she went to her toaster oven and pulled out the small package of brownies. She had seen them at the deli when she went to the store the previous day. As hard as she was trying to stay away from all that luscious chocolate, the package had called out to her so loudly; she just couldn't walk away from it. She had put it in the toaster oven, which she didn't use very often, thinking that if she didn't see them, maybe she would forget they were there. Shelby had deluded herself about many things through the years, but she knew she wouldn't forget where those delicious chocolate and peanut butter brownies were. But it had been worth a try. Now she was very thankful that they were there. She knew that she relied on food more often than she should for comfort, but right at this minute, she needed all the comfort she could get, so she opened the oven door and pulled out the two remaining brownies and sat them on a paper towel. She then got a glass of cold milk from the refrigerator and took them both back to the couch with her. Charlie was right beside her, looking hopeful that she would share the brownies. Shelby obliged and after their treats, they both settled back into their comfortable position on the couch. The memories that Shelby hadn't wanted to relive now came flooding back to her.

* * *

For her, a person who liked to hold and be held, and swooned whenever she was held in Todd's arms, the fact that Todd had seldom touched her at all in their last years together was the cause of the anguish and heartbreak she had a hard time dealing with. He could have punched her and it would have hurt less than going without the intimacy of his touch. Every time she walked towards Todd desiring to be held, he would raise his arms to stop her from getting close to him and if she did manage to get close, he would literally push her away. The continuous rejection she was being subjected to on top of the ever present insecurity she had, shattered any remaining amount of confidence or self worth she had.

It finally got to the point where the hurt and confusion Shelby was experiencing became too much for her and she could no longer hide the fact that something was terribly wrong in her life. Her friend Karen, whom she had grown close to over the past few years, encouraged Shelby to open up and tell her what was going on. Shelby and Todd had come to know Karen and her husband Tom well as their son's were involved in the same sports through the years and they all spent many evenings together at practices and games.

Shelby was initially very reluctant to tell Karen or anyone what was going on between her and Todd. As silly as it sounded, she thought that saying it out loud might make it true. She also didn't want to admit to anyone that her life, which was outwardly so stable and happy, was actually full of turmoil and despair. But, Shelby finally opened up to Karen and as she began to bear her soul to her friend, the burden she had carried on her back seemed to become lighter. She had someone to confide in now, to support her by giving her a shoulder to lean on. As they worked together in the same building, they were able to spend their morning and afternoon breaks together talking. This time they spent together gave Shelby a chance to vent her heartache and helped her to realize that she didn't have any deficiencies. Todd's treatment was just making her feel inadequate and insignificant.

On top of being there for her to talk too, Karen also invited Shelby and Todd to come to her house and play cards with her and Tom. Karen thought that maybe if they were able to get out together and have some fun, maybe Todd would start enjoying spending time with Shelby again.

Shelby was still willing to try anything she could to rekindle the love that she thought Todd once felt for her. She held onto the hope that if she loved him deeply enough and didn't give him any reason to leave her, then eventually he would be remorseful about how badly he had treated her and would realize how much she meant to him.

* * *

Chapter Seventeen

Todd never did fall back in love with Shelby. Although it was almost impossible for her to comprehend, Shelby continued to wonder whether he had ever really loved her at all. Being disillusioned about something she believed in so strongly, and for so many years, was overwhelmingly earth shattering to Shelby. Had her love for Todd blinded her to the point where she didn't see or think rationally? Had she been so cleverly manipulated that her perception of their entire marriage was distorted?

Whichever the case was, Shelby recalled with fondness, the event that occurred that helped her change the perception she had about herself. One memorable night turned Shelby's life around. She began to feel more positive about herself because one person, who sensed how she was being treated, took the initiative to remind her that she was still an attractive and desirable woman. Because of that one person on that one night, Shelby finally realized that she deserved to be treated better than she had been by Todd.

It was the night of the Sheriff Department's Christmas party where the drinks flowed freely and the dance music was vibrating. While Todd ignored Shelby the entire evening, Shelby sat quietly at the table where the Sheriff and Undersheriff sat along with their wives. They were always so nice to Shelby and made her feel welcome although she wasn't quite sure whether the kindness was sincere or whether they were simply being nice to her because she was Todd's wife. But regardless, they were very warm and hospitable. The music was loud, making conversation difficult, so Shelby simply sat back graciously and watched the spectacle around her. Seeing the steady traffic of party-goers repeatedly returning to the bar, it didn't surprise Shelby that there was an abundant amount of frolicking and indescreationery behavior.   Shelby smiled, wondering how embarrassed those people would be when they found out how they acted while under the influence of all that holiday cheer.

As she sat there, sitting in amused distraction, one of Todd's co-workers, a member of the DEA came and sat next to her. He sat close so that they could hold a conversation and still be heard over the volume of the music, and they talked for a long time. Not about anything specific, they just talked: about their jobs, her children, and the latest gossip. It had been a long time since Todd had taken the time, and showed the desire, to carry on a simple conversation with her, that she assumed that she must be uninteresting, boring, and dull.

As the evening progressed, they were not only talking, but Shelby found herself laughing. She was actually having a great time. Then it got even better when Will asked her to dance several times. Shelby loved to dance and in years past, she and Todd had spent hours together on the dance floor on the infrequent opportunities they had to go out. But lately when they did have the chance, like that night, Todd was very interested in dancing, but not with her. Todd's only explanation was that although he really wasn't in the mood to dance that night, he was just trying to be friendly when the other women asked him to dance.

Despite the fact that Todd had brought her to the party and left her to sit by herself in a corner, she had a truly enjoyable evening. She had more fun that night than she had had in a very long time. If she hadn't been married, she might have taken Will's friendliness as a flirtatious advance, but, as she was, she saw it as it actually was, a man who was alone at a party, enjoying his evening with a woman who in essence was alone too.

After that night, Shelby decided to pick herself up by the bootstraps and do whatever she needed to do to bring peace and happiness back into her life.

Shelby didn't have any idea where to begin, but she was finally realizing that the way Todd treated her was no longer acceptable. He didn't seem to have the capacity, or desire, to encourage and support her. Nor did he make her feel admired and loved. She was just going to have to take some steps on her own to pick up her shattered ego from the floor where Todd had been kicking it around.

Between the needs of her children, her job, and having a high-maintenance husband, Shelby had never actually found much time to think about herself … let alone act on it. After years of putting her wants and needs last, consciously thinking about doing something solely for herself wasn't a mindset that she was accustomed to or comfortable with. Shelby decided that the first thing she needed to concentrate on was her appearance. She really needed a pick-me-up. Over time, Shelby had put on extra weight and spent more time in comfortable yet unappealing sweatpants. And due to neglect, her hair was unstyled and unbecoming.

Shelby knew she was ready for a make-over: physically and emotionally. She told herself that if she looked more attractive maybe she would feel better about herself. No, Shelby realized, that wasn't it. She just wanted Todd to notice her and to be attracted to her like he once had been. She wanted him to look at her with pride and joy. She had tried everything she could think of to win his heart back, but it had all seemingly failed. She had prayed for guidance and felt sure that this was her last hope of success.

P.L. John

Shelby took her portable CD player and the 'Wide Open Spaces' CD of the Dixie Chicks with her down to the basement. Her exercise bike sat in the corner, dusty and discarded like all the other items that were stored down there. The basement itself wasn't glum, the floors had been painted gray and the cement walls had been painted white. Well, two of the walls had been painted. Todd still hadn't finished the other two. Maybe someday … when he had time.

There were two high windows on each of the front and rear walls that let in the bright sunshine. At night there were four overhead lights that chased away the darkness from the corners.

It was a place that now suited her needs. She could play the soulful music, sing along with the heart-wrenching lyrics, and let her tears flow freely as she feverishly peddled. She pressed to extend the length of time she spent on the bike each time she got on it. She was driven; she had a target to aim for and a purpose that bordered between life and death for her heart. No matter how positive she tried to be, the fact remained that she was losing, or had already lost, her husband. The marriage that she had revolved her life around was all but over. The tears she shed was the release of the pain her heart was feeling.

The invisible miles she rode on the bike seemed to be benefiting Shelby in more ways than physically. She discovered that she felt somewhat renewed and strengthened each time she climbed back up the basement steps. The invigorating workout seemed to be as good for her soul as it was for her body. She soon started to look toned and walked with her head held a little higher although Todd still walked out of the room when she walked into it.

210

Still trying to hang onto the few remaining threads that held their marriage together, Shelby and Todd continued to go to Karen and Tom's frequently to play cards. Todd seemed animated and relaxed on these evenings. The problem was that he didn't talk to Shelby on the way to or from Karen's. He also became insistent that they go there four or five nights a week.

Todd had recently been promoted to detective and after years of working the night shift, the schedule change that Shelby had longed for had finally occurred. He was now working during the daytime. Now that Todd was able to spend evenings home, he thought of every reason imaginable not to be there. At least when they went to Karen's, she was with Todd. Otherwise, he would just hop in the patrol car after receiving a page, stating that he needed to go to the office concerning one investigation or another.

Over a matter of a few months, Shelby started feeling uncomfortable at Todd's continued eagerness to go to Karen and Tom's so frequently. Karen began to lose an incredible amount of weight and she and Todd candidly told each other very sexually explicit jokes throughout the card games. There was a tension between them that couldn't be ignored. They made Shelby feel like she was invisible, like it was only the two of them at the table. Shelby would occasionally look at Tom questioningly, but he either didn't seem to notice, or didn't want to let anyone know that he noticed the connection that was occurring right before their eyes.

As their social visits continued, Shelby became outwardly disturbed when Karen even began to cut Todd's hair. While Shelby sat in the living room or outside in the lawn chair visiting with Tom, Todd and Karen would be in the kitchen as she trimmed his hair with the clippers. Shelby couldn't understand this at all. Todd was never even charged for the haircut he received at the town barber, so why was it necessary for Karen to cut his hair?

When Shelby questioned Todd about this and told him how uncomfortable she was becoming, Todd blew up at her.

"Here you go again, becoming jealous about nothing. Don't you dare say anything to either Karen or Tom about this. I don't ever seem to be able to talk to any woman without you imagining something more is going on. God Shelby, sometimes I think you're crazy. I'm going to continue visiting Karen whether you want me to or not. I'm not giving up good friends just because you're acting so stupid."

As if to purposely defy Shelby, Todd went to have coffee with Karen on Saturday mornings, times when Shelby knew that Tom was at work. It was as if Todd was daring Shelby to say anything, knowing she couldn't do anything to stop what was going on. Shelby's gut told her that something inappropriate was going on between them. She knew that if they weren't already involved, they soon would be. The worst part was that it was all occurring under the pretence of the women being best friends. No one questioned it when they saw Todd and Karen together at ball games, which Shelby couldn't attend because of their children's conflicting sport schedules. Frequently Jonelle's volleyball games were played at the same time as James' football games, but in a different town. Todd always insisted that he attend James' games and stood with his constant companion Karen.

Looking back on it, Shelby wondered if people really did question it and talked about it amongst themselves, but never dared say anything to Shelby. They must have realized how devastated she would be. They probably figured she already knew about it or that it wasn't their place to say anything. Shelby recalled now that there were comments made to her jokingly that pointed out that Karen and Todd appeared like more of a couple than she and Todd did. Shelby had laughed along with them, giving them the sense that it was silly to think that Shelby's best friend and her husband would be involved. They just figured that Shelby must really trust Todd to be comfortable with the situation, especially when they would see Karen and Todd together in her car at a game whenever the weather was inclement. Or, had they just thought she was blind and foolish not to see what was going on under her nose? Whatever the case, Shelby eventually broke off her friendship with Karen, a decision that had incensed Todd.

"Do you know how bad Karen and Tom feel about what you're accusing us of doing? They don't deserve to be dragged down by your crazy innuendos. I'm not breaking off my friendship with them just because you're jealous. This happens every time I make friends with someone," he said angrily as he stormed out the back door.

Shelby sat down dejectedly in the dining room chair that she had been standing next to. She hung her head and rested it in her hands after raising her elbows to the table. Defeated again. It didn't seem to matter what she said or did to try and pull their marriage out of the gutter. She had tried and done everything that was in her power to do. Everything had failed.

Shelby felt crushed and finally realized that there was nothing more she could do. She lifted her head slowly from her opened hands. She closed her eyes tightly, entwined her fingers and laid her forehead gently on her hands, balled together in prayer.

"Dear God, I pray in your name through Your son Jesus Christ and ask that You hear my prayer. Forgive me for my many sins dear Lord, for things that I have done that I shouldn't have, for things that didn't do that I should have, for things that I've said that I shouldn't have, for things that I didn't say but should have and for things that I've thought that I shouldn't have. I need Your help Lord. I need the burden of this marriage taken off of my shoulders. I can't bear the weight by myself any longer. I need Your guidance dear Lord. Please tell me, should I continue this fight to save my marriage? Is there something else I should do or say? If there is, let me know what it is because I don't have any more ideas. Do I just let go, Lord? Do I just accept that my marriage is really over? That I've lost Todd forever? Please help me Lord, please. In Your name I pray. Amen."

Shelby pulled herself slowly from the chair and walked over to the kitchen sink and finished washing the pans she had cooked dinner in. Jonelle was going to bring James home after the varsity basketball game they went to. James was on the junior high team and couldn't wait until he played at the high school level. Jonelle went just to support the team. Many of them had come to watch her varsity volleyball games and she wanted to support them in the playoffs. They would be home soon, Shelby thought to herself. She had to dry her tears and pull herself together before they walked through the door.

Weeks and months passed. Shelby didn't know whether any of the kids knew that their parent's marriage was in such sad shape. She suspected they did as the tension had to be thick in the air, but she had tried very hard to keep the troubles contained so that the kids weren't distracted or forced to deal with the pain and disillusionment that Shelby had to deal with on a daily basis. Fortunately Hayleigh was away at college now, so Shelby was thankful that at least one of their children wasn't exposed to the wall that had been built between her and Todd. Shelby just hoped that Jonelle and James weren't being affected by any of this either. Since Todd's presence in their home had always been scarce, she was hoping that they hadn't found his absence unusual. If she could just keep her emotions under control, maybe she could spare them the heartache that she felt.

Shelby went to work and once again felt invigorated. She truly loved her new job. She had recently obtained an accounting position with the county, but in a different office complex, a mile down the road from the Sheriff's Department where Todd worked. Since she'd started her new job, there hadn't been a day that she wasn't eager to get there. The uneasiness she had felt working in the same building as Karen and the stress of having additional job duties assigned to her had made her contemplate looking for another job. She had been fortunate that this new position she had just been hired for became available at the same time she made the decision to start looking for another job. It was as if the position opened just for her, as if it was meant to be. Shelby felt confident in her ability to work with numbers so she eased into the job duties without any trouble. And, the people she worked with were so nice. There wasn't one person that she didn't get along with. It made her home life with Todd bearable. Her children and her work gave Shelby the purpose she needed to keep going. And work was her escape. Her co-workers liked her, respected the work she did and thought of her as an asset. Sometimes Shelby was hesitant to leave work at the end of the day. What did she have to go home to? The kids would be at practice, and even though Todd's work day would be over, he wouldn't be there. It would be another day for her to wonder where he was, who he was with and what he was doing. It tortured her; in fact Shelby didn't know how much longer she could live like this.

By the time Shelby pulled into the driveway after returning home from work on a Friday afternoon, she knew what she had to do. Leave. She knew her parents would welcome her into their home and since James and Jonelle were spending the night at friends, she didn't have to worry about what to tell them until the next day. She immediately went into her bedroom and pulled the suitcase from the closet. Her hands shook, her heart was full of despair and the tears streamed down her cheeks, but she knew this was the only thing left for her to do. She couldn't deal with Todd's harsh comments and his dejection any more.

Just as she had finished putting the clothes she would need in the suitcase, Todd walked into the bedroom, pulling off his tie. He glared at her disdainfully as he always did and then stopped cold in his track as soon as he saw the suitcase on the bed.

"What's going on? Are you planning on going some where?" he sneered at her.

"I'm leaving, Todd. I'm going to go down to mom & dad's so I can be with people that like me and want to be around me," Shelby said with a mixture of pain and resolve.

Todd walked to the closet to hang his tie up on the tie rack inside of it and shook his head. With his back still towards her, acting as if this news was of little concern to him he said, "Shelby, you're not even making any sense.

What are the kids going to think when they get home and find out you're spending the night at your parents?"

"I'm not just going to spend tonight there. Todd, I'm leaving you," she said with a firmness that even surprised herself.

Todd turned around and looked at her. The pissy look that was normally on his face was gone. In its place was a look of utter shock. One that told Shelby that he realized that she wasn't kidding, that she wasn't going to take this any longer.

"You wouldn't leave the kids," Todd said in a low voice, and expression of confusion slowly replacing his initial look of shock. He took one step toward her, hesitated, and then asked. "Why are you doing this?"

"You're right; leaving the kids is the hardest thing I've ever had to do in my life." Shelby looked down, trying to hold back her tears and remain strong and firm. "I'll talk to them tomorrow. Todd, I can't live with you any longer. You don't even like me and I can't take being treated so badly anymore. I'm going to go live with someone that enjoys having me around. This is the kids' home. Just because I can't live here any more doesn't give me the right to take them away from it. They can come visit me as much as they want."

Todd looked at Shelby with a blank expression on his face. Then, as he realized how serious Shelby was he said. "No, the kids aren't going to understand if you're not here. Why don't I just go? I could say I had to work."

"No, Todd, we're not going to pretend that you're working and that everything is fine any more," Shelby said, long suppressed anger making her voice harsh. "Things aren't fine and I can't act as if they are any more. I know you have political aspirations and it's been important for it to appear like you're a loving husband and father. I know that's the only reason you've stayed with me all these years. You've been able to do whatever you've wanted to do and still maintain the illusion of a happy family man. It's been a perfect setup for you. Well, I can't live like that any more, so I'll leave. I'll be the bad guy. I'll be the woman who left her husband and children. You won't ever have to deal with the repercussions of leaving your family. Just let me go Todd. Since you're always gone to have coffee on Saturday mornings, I'll come home and explain things to the kids while you're gone. I'll break it to them as gently as possible."

And with that, Shelby zipped the suitcase up, pulled it off the bed and walked out of the bedroom door and out of the house. She had already called her parents earlier and asked if she could come and spend some time there. They hadn't asked any questions, they had simply said. "You're welcome any time, come on down."

Shelby got there, her stomach rolling as if she were going to vomit any minute. She carried her suitcase upstairs into the spare bedroom and slowly sank down onto the bed.

* * *

Chapter Eighteen

Shelby felt like she was afloat on a stormy sea. Though she had experienced some difficult situations in her life, she had never before felt this empty, this hollow and so full of upheaval. Life was revolving all around her, but she no longer felt a part of it. In a matter of hours, life as she had known it was gone. It had been unraveling for a long time, but finally, the end of the rope had arrived. She felt as if her feet had been knocked out from beneath her and she couldn't imagine how the kids were going to react. How would they possibly be able to deal with this? Shelby fretfully worried whether this news would obscure the perception they had about the reality of their lives … as it had her.

Everything that she had tried to do to make her children feel secure and grounded was about to be destroyed. They were about to find out that their parents were separating and that their mother had moved out of their home - all on a Friday night that had started out like every other Friday night of their lives. How would she tell them? What would she say?

The following morning, Shelby drove back up the hill to her home, which they had moved into only a few years earlier. It sat overlooking the valley where the quaint village and her parent's home was located. Her thoughts were scattered and her mind was a little fuzzy. She had finally fallen to sleep in exhaustion during the early morning hours, but had awoken fitfully from a nightmare which she now couldn't recall. Todd would be gone by the time she got to the house and the kids were expected home soon. She knew it was time to explain to her children that their family was about to be ripped apart. The task was daunting and her heart was racing with trepidation.

As she pulled into the long driveway, it dawned on her that this home of hers, the one she loved and derived so much peace from, had never been a place that Todd considered home. It made her wonder how a person could be so enthusiastic about planning a new home, then, completely lose interest once there. He left many painting and building projects unfinished, just as their marriage now was.

There were a lot of things Shelby didn't understand and couldn't explain. She slowly climbed the steps onto the deck and entered the house through the back door. As she walked into the kitchen, she stopped momentarily, looking around, to soak in the beauty and warmth of the large kitchen with its many oak cabinets.

Shelby, feeling unbalanced and in total confusion about her decision to leave everything that mattered to her in life, walked into the living room and sat nervously on the couch. She rested her travel mug on her knees and gripped it tightly, trying to stop her shaking hands. She was feeling overwhelmed by the enormity of the task that lay ahead of her. Tears started to stream down her face and for a fleeting moment, she almost convinced herself to run back to her car and let Todd be the one to explain to their kids what was going on.

No, she couldn't do that to the children she loved so dearly. She needed to be honest and up front with them. They deserved that from her, just as she had deserved Todd's respect and honesty. She had to pull herself together and figure out what words she could possibly say that would explain any of the whirlwind that they were now in the middle of.

Jonelle and James finally arrived home and as expected they had a great deal of trouble comprehending what she was telling them. Shelby explained as gently as possible, that she and Todd were having some serious problems and that she was going to stay at grandma and grandpa's so that she could have time to figure out what to do next. Shelby soothed their fretful tears, reassured them how very much she loved them and encouraged them to come and spend as much time with her as they wanted. Instinctively, she could see and feel that they understood the gravity of what was occurring. They were upset, but admitted that they had been more aware of the strain between their parents than Shelby had realized. Therefore, this news that she broke to them wasn't a complete surprise and therefore wasn't as devastating as it could have been. What was shocking to them was the fact that their mom was the one leaving. They never thought she would be the one to leave her family and home. Shelby could only reassure them that she was not leaving them. That she would be there for them just as she always had been. She just needed some time to sort things through.

On her drive back to her parent's house, Shelby thought about how confused and bewildered Jonelle and James must be. As soon as she entered the familiar house where she had been raised, she immediately went to the phone, called Hayleigh, and broke the news to her too. As much as she wished it to be so, she could no longer make everything alright and she could no longer protect her children from the realities of this upsetting turn of events. Shelby knew that she had made the only decision she could make and for the first time, in a very long time, she had to think of her own needs right now. It had been a hard choice to make, but Shelby thought she was finally ready to let go – let go of not only the man she'd always thought of as the love of her life, but also to let go of the marriage she'd been sure would endure until death parted them.

It was early afternoon on the following day when Shelby received a phone call from Todd. She didn't know whether she was prepared to talk to him yet, but hesitantly nodded assent when Louise asked Shelby if she wanted to talk to him. She reached for the receiver that Louise reluctantly handed her and slowly lifted it to her ear.

"Hello?" Shelby asked meekly. The onslaught of emotional confusion making her feel disorientated.

"Hi, Shelb," Todd said, sounding uncharacteristically nervous. "How are you?"

Shelby took a deep breath to calm her racing heart. "I'm doing all right I guess. How are the kids?"

"They're a wreck," he said disheartenly. "That's why I'm calling. They don't understand what's happening and they miss you terribly." He paused a second, probably to regain his composure or to find the right words. "Would you please come up home and eat dinner with us this afternoon? I'm going to make some goulash and I know it would mean a lot to the kids if you would come see them."

Shelby bit her lower lip, her heart breaking from the emotional pain her children were enduring. She didn't know what to do or say. Although she really wasn't ready to see Todd yet, she knew the kids must be suffering and she had to do whatever she could to help them get through this.

"Shelby?" Todd said in a worried tone. "Are you there?"

"Yeah Todd," Shelby exhaled heavily as she squeezed her eyes shut. "I'm here. Tell the kids I'll come up in a little while. I'd like to see them. I miss them."

"That's great," Todd said enthusiastically. "Come up any time you want to. You can visit with the kids and maybe we can get a chance to talk after dinner."

"Todd, I'll come up because I'm worried about the kids. I don't know if I'm ready to talk to you yet."

"Okay, okay," Todd said nervously, as if she might change her mind. "Just come up for dinner and talk with the kids, alright?"

"Alright," Shelby said quickly. "I'll be up in about an hour, bye."

Shelby used both hands to carefully place the receiver back on the phone then leaned heavily on it. She heard the wooden stand beneath it creak as it supported her. She closed her eyes and exhaled the breath that she seemed to have been holding. His voice, his very being, evoked the love and passion she still felt for him. The humbleness of that voice weakened her resolve to walk away from him. No, she shook her head. She couldn't back down now. It had taken a great deal of heartache and a long period of time for her to come to the decision that this was the only option left for her. To give in to her heart now would only give Todd permission to continue to treat her as he had been. As impossibly difficult as this decision had been, she couldn't change her mind now.

Shelby knew her mother was concerned about the conversation she had just had with Todd. She straightened up from the hallway telephone table and went into the kitchen to tell Louise about Todd's invitation to dinner. Then, Shelby went upstairs to wash up and change her clothes: anything to keep her from pacing and fretting about the upcoming visit with her family.

Soon it was time for her journey to her home. Shelby was nervous, almost to the point of breathlessness. Her hands shook on the steering wheel and her heart raced as she drove the short distance from her parent's house. As she pulled into the driveway and walked up the back steps of their deck, Shelby steadied her emotions. She was determined to show her children that she was alright so that they wouldn't worry needlessly about her. She also wanted to be a source of strength and comfort for them as she always had been and would always try to be.

As she walked into the kitchen, she was greeted by Jonelle and James. She smiled warmly and hugged them tightly, trying with every fiber of her being to chase away the sadness from their eyes. Todd stood back and only advanced into the kitchen, where Shelby still stood, after the kids had broken away from the tight embrace. Shelby stared at him and without being hostile, made it quite clear by the way she looked, that he wasn't to advance any closer to her. As difficult as it was to keep the man she had always loved at arms length, she knew that her resolve and strength would drain away quickly if she stared into his dark eyes or allowed him to pull her into his arms. She needed to be strong.

The dinner and afternoon went as well as could be expected. On top of the ever present tension in the air, there was also uneasiness as everyone searched for the right thing to say or do. Todd had seemed very pleased with himself for making the meal and seemed a little mystified that Shelby wasn't complimenting him on a job well done. If truth could be told, Shelby secretly wondered whether Jonelle had made the dinner. Besides cooking an occasional Sunday breakfast, Todd had never been one to be inclined to even open a can of soup for himself when he was hungry.

After they had picked at their plates for what seemed like an eternity, Shelby and the kids went into the living room where they sat and talked while Todd went outdoors. The kids didn't question her decision, seek answers, or make her feel guilty. They just wanted and needed some resemblance of normalcy back in their lives for a few hours. They simply talked about anything and everything besides what was going on with Shelby and Todd and as the afternoon came to an end, they made plans to go down to the river the following weekend to fish.

Since the kids were now more relaxed, Shelby knew that it was time for her visit to come to an end. It was time for her to leave her home and family once again. Shelby stood up to prepare for their solemn good-byes when Todd came back into the house. He walked into the living room and stepped hesitantly towards Shelby. As she turned around and looked towards him, she noticed that his eyes, which seconds before had been looking downward, were now fixed directly onto hers. She couldn't help but notice the pain and sorrow they contained or, judging from the dark shadows, the fact that it appeared he had also had a sleepless night.

"Hey, Shelb. Could we talk for just a few minutes before you leave?"

To Shelby, he sounded as nervous and unsure of himself as he had been when he arrived at her apartment door the evening after they had first gone hunting. There was an uncertainty about him that made him appear vulnerable. Part of her wanted to reach her arms out to him, pull him into her arms and tell him everything was going to be alright. The part of her that was well aware of her weaknesses where Todd was concerned backed up a step and looked downward toward the floor to avoid eye contact with him.

"Please, Shelb. I think we need to talk."

Shelby knew it couldn't be avoided. They did need to talk. So, she looked up at him and nodded her head. "Alright," she said softly. She took a deep breath and expelled it along with the nervousness that tried to seep back into her. She knew she had to be strong. She couldn't let her emotions get the best of her this time. Shelby knew she had to give Todd a chance to say what was on his mind, but she couldn't let her love for him sway the decision she had made.

Todd tilted his head towards their bedroom to indicate where they should go and talk. Shelby walked resolutely towards the room, not wanting to acknowledge the intimacy of the location where their discussion would be held. Todd closed the door and they sat next to each other on the edge of the bed. Shelby blocked out everything around her and waited for Todd to say what he wanted to say.

Todd reached out for her hands, but Shelby instinctively pulled hers back away from his. Todd therefore pulled his back too, lowered them into his lap and clasped them together. He appeared nervous, as is he was summoning up the courage he needed to plead his case.

Looking down at his hands he said, "Shelb, I know I've been a real asshole." He took a deep breath and continued. "I guess I've been restless or bored. I don't really know. But whatever the reason, I shouldn't have treated you as badly as I did and I'm sorry."

Shelby didn't know how to respond. Todd had never apologized to her before, never. He had never said, "I'm sorry" nor ever given any hint that he thought what he had said or done was wrong. Shelby was not prepared in any way to hear those words come out of Todd's mouth. No two words had ever sounded so sweet to her. Because Shelby knew how much it must have cost him to say them, she knew that he must mean them. It almost made everything that had happened even harder to deal with. Tears started running silently down her cheeks. The gratitude and relief she felt when she received the apology from Todd confused her and seemed to take away the strength of the fortitude she had been resolved to hold on to. Her heart warmed to the point where she was willing to believe he actually meant what he was saying, and therefore, she accepted his apology.

"Shelb, I really don't want you to leave me. I promise you, things will be better between us. Please," Todd said as he looked pleadingly into her eyes. "Will you please come home?"

Shelby looked at Todd deeply, searching to see if she could find any tell-tale clues that would help her determine whether the words that he was saying matched the feelings in his heart. His eyes were filled with unshed tears and his face was drawn, as if he were in physical pain.

She hadn't even remotely considered the possibility that Todd would want her to stay. She thought he'd jump at this golden opportunity to end the marriage. She had given him the 'out' she was sure he'd wanted for a very long time. Why was it, that now that she was willing to let him go, he suddenly wanted her to stay? Her heart that had been broken seemed to be feeling more whole, as if it were being glued together and repaired. Although she didn't want to let all of her defenses down, she did feel nervously excited that Todd still wanted her. She felt encouraged that there might still be a chance that they could save their marriage.

But, there was more she needed to know ..

"Todd, before I can think about that, I need you to be completely honest me about something," she said resolutely, her face relaying the seriousness of how she felt. "Please tell me the truth Todd. Are you having an affair?"

Todd seemed to be totally taken aback by this question. By the look on his face, Shelby could tell that it was the last question he expected to hear: that he was completely dumbfounded by what she had asked. While through the years Shelby had admittedly expressed uneasiness about several women or situations Todd was involved with, she had never had the courage to come right out and point blank ask him that question before.

"No Shelb," he said emphatically. "Honestly I'm not." He looked down at his hands and continued although more subdued. "I thought about it. In fact I had actually been trying to find someone that would be interested. But, I swear nothing has happened and I promise I will never even think about it again."

Shelby tried to take this all in. On one hand, it was very hard to hear Todd admit to his desire to have an affair. On the other hand, he had come right out and admitted he was tempted but didn't go through with it. Shelby truly felt that he was at last being totally honest with her.

"Are you sure about this, Todd? Do you promise that things are going to change? Because I can't live like this any more," Shelby said, her voice deep with emotion and her heart almost afraid to hope it might be true.

"Yes. I want us to stay married and I promise I'll change. Please come back home, okay?"

Shelby couldn't help but feel elated. She wanted to throw herself into Todd's arms and kiss him passionately, but something inside her told her she should go slow and not throw caution to the wind.

"Okay, Todd," Shelby said slowly. Before she could say anything else, she saw Todd's eyes brightened and a victorious smile spread over his face, but still, she continued. "I'll come back for a few days, but I need to see how things go before I make my final decision."

The expression on Todd's face changed from glee to utter shock and confusion at Shelby's conditional agreement. Shelby almost saw the hope of victory turn into the pain of defeat in a fraction of a second. She had Todd's attention and she wasn't about to let him off the hook quite as easily as he probably thought he would.

* * *

Chapter Nineteen

As the weeks passed, Shelby was pleasantly surprised to see that her relationship with Todd was steadily improving. Todd really started putting some effort into 'fixing' what had ailed in their marriage, namely his involvement in it. He started taking an interest in Shelby's life. They discussed what happened during her day as well as what happened in his and they went out to have a drink and dinner by themselves at least once a week. It was the first time in many years that they had gone out on a date. Todd even surprised Shelby on her birthday, taking her to an Italian restaurant on the lake that she had always wanted to go to. It was the first time Todd had ever done something just for the sole purpose of making Shelby happy, so the enormity of the occasion didn't escape unnoticed by her.

They weren't in blissful happiness, but they were beginning to have a relationship that had substance. Todd was more respectful to Shelby. He was kinder and seemed more content. It was as if there had previously been someone or something that was interfering in their relationship and now, whoever or whatever it was, was gone. Todd arrived home at the end of each work day and even though his first priority when he got home was to read the newspaper, his presence was welcomed by Shelby and the kids.

The only occurrence which made Shelby uneasy was Todd's newfound interest in jogging. Although she had never once seen him dawn a pair of running shoes at home, he enthusiastically packed his gym bag and went into the office early at least three mornings a week so he could go running with the Undersheriff. Even though he didn't have to be at work until 9:00 in the morning, 8:00 at the earliest, he would consistently rise before the light of day and leave the house by 5:00 a.m.

As hard as Shelby tried to chase away her uneasiness and underlying fear that there was something more than jogging going on, she couldn't substantiate it. She felt ashamed for questioning his simple desire to exercise especially because he was making so many strides forward in his attentiveness towards their marriage. She was afraid that she was allowing herself to fall back into the old pattern of being insecure and suspicious. She tried, but she couldn't suppress the unfounded fears - they were still there. That ever present feeling in her gut that told her something wasn't right had returned and Shelby didn't like it at all.

When Shelby finally revealed her uneasiness to Todd, he expressed how disappointed he was that she had regressed to where her trust in him was wavering again. But he wasn't defensive or critical like he previously had been. Instead, he reassured her that the only thing he was doing was running. He also told her that if she felt more comfortable, she could call the Undersheriff or the dispatchers any time she wanted. They would all be able to confirm that he was there. But, the one thing he wasn't willing to do was to stop running with Mike in the morning.

Shelby knew she would never call either the dispatchers or the Undersheriff to check up on Todd. So, she consciously decided to just push down the nagging doubts that kept trying to pop up. Instead, she decided for once and for all to put her trust in Todd.

With her fears put to rest and her mind at ease, Shelby began to relax and enjoy life. Whether she was at home, at one of the kid's games or attending any one of the numerous political functions or departmental gatherings with Todd, Shelby enjoyed herself and had fun.

Late fall arrived, as did the cold, brisk air and the occasional snowfall. The weather was seldom conducive to jogging and soon Todd began to act restless again. Along with the restlessness, Shelby sensed that Todd was pulling away from her and the kids again. By his sullen behavior, Shelby instinctively knew that he was once again dissatisfied with his home life.

Her uneasiness was substantiated when they attended a retirement party for a long-time dispatcher at the department. They arrived at the party a little early, so Todd and Shelby went into the bar area to get a cocktail. Shelby recognized almost everyone there and warmly greeted them all. Just before heading into the dining room with their drinks, Shelby noticed the arrival of two women as they took off their jackets in the entryway. She recognized them both, and although the two women worked at the county building, neither of them worked in the Sheriff department, so she was a little surprised to see them there. Shelby had known one of the women, Carrie, for many years. She also knew that Carrie was pulling out all of the stops in her attempts to pursue a relationship with a lieutenant in the department. Since he was there that night with his wife, Shelby shuddered as she thought about what might happen. Shelby only knew the other woman, Sherry because she worked in the county's Information Services department and on occasion, came to the building where Shelby worked to correct a problem with a computer or printer.

Shelby didn't think much more about it until dinner was finished and people got up from their seats to go mingle. While Shelby was visiting with the wives of the investigators that Todd worked with, she couldn't help noticing that as Todd made his rounds, he kept returning to where Sherry and Carrie were sitting. Shelby wondered if indeed there were problems arising between Carrie and the lieutenant and that Todd might be trying to head her off at the path.

When Todd finally made his way back to where Shelby sat, Carrie and Sherry were with him and they all sat across the table from Shelby, one of the women on each side of Todd. They were very intoxicated by this time and Sherry was giggling and teasing Todd insistently, seemingly unconcerned that his wife was sitting right across from them, forced to watch the entire escapade. Shelby finally started feeling unnerved when Sherry conveniently slopped her drink on the front of Todd's shirt. While giggling her apologies to Todd, she unknotted his tie and pulled it suggestively off his collar.

Shelby could see that Todd, who had also been drinking a lot more than he normally did, wasn't able to conceal his enjoyment of the seductive performance, and laughed heartily, his face flushed with dark excitement.

As if finally remembering that Shelby was seated with them, Todd and Sherry drew back from each other. Sherry's eyes were slightly unfocused behind the thick lenses of her glasses as she gave Shelby a malicious smile that somehow managed to convey both pity and triumph. Sherry again apologized to Todd for spilling the drink on his tie, folded the tie, and told him she would have it dry-cleaned for him as she tucked it into her purse. Sherry, Todd, and Carrie all laughed at the incident and then the two women excused themselves.

Shelby sat in her seat half stunned, half seething with anger. As Todd sat across from her laughing and shrugging off the incident, Shelby could see his chest fill with haughty pride. She was also sure that his pride wasn't the only thing of Todd's that had been swelling. She could see by the gleam in his eyes and the smirk that had formed on his lips, that he was indeed aroused by Sherry's suggestive performance.

The heartbreaking part of the whole incident was that Shelby felt their relationship had come so far and, in a matter of minutes, all of Todd's concerns for her feelings were shattered by the promise of cheap sex dangling under his nose.

Shelby was still reeling on the spectacle made by Todd and Sherry at the retirement dinner when a couple of weeks later, Sherry's name arose again in a conversation Shelby wasn't supposed to hear. Shelby and Todd were at an inauguration party for the newly elected District Attorney. Shelby wasn't attending only as Todd's spouse this time. She had actively and vigorously campaigned for the new DA as he was running against the attorney who had botched her case so badly in court. Shelby had gone to choose a couple hors d'oeuvres to snack on and had moved on to the punch bowl to fill her cup, when she noticed a lively conversation was being held between the Sheriff, Undersheriff and Todd. They were within hearing range and were discussing who should be hired to replace the secretary for the detective bureau when the current secretary retired. It soon became apparent that they didn't know Shelby was nearby as a guttural laugh announced.

".. We all know who Todd would like to have as the new secretary .. Sherry."

The sound of laughter and back-slapping faded into the distance as Shelby slowly turned and walked in the opposite direction.

As if nervous whether anyone had overheard the comment the Sheriff had made, Todd looked around, scanning the crowd to see who was close by. A short distance away, Todd saw Shelby walking slowly away. Her head was bent down slightly, as if to avoid the eyes of those passing her. Her shoulders were slumped forward as if she was downtrodden or had just had the wind knocked out of her. Instinctively Todd knew that she had overheard the conversation. Out of everyone in that room, the one person he feared the most would hear the comment did indeed hear it. He knew the festivity of the evening was over and walked hastily towards her.

When Shelby reached the doorway of the reception hall, she glanced back and saw Todd coming. Their eyes met and she could see the look of desperation on his face. When he caught up with her outside the doorway, he gently grabbed her elbow to try and stop her. Before he had time to say anything, Shelby cut him off. In a voice depleted of energy and void of emotion she said.

"I'm not feeling too well. I'm ready to leave."

Nothing else needed to be said. Their exit was hasty and just as inconspicuous as it had been at the retirement party. While driving away, Shelby finally released the penned up anger and hurt she was feeling as she yelled.

"How could you? Damn you." Shelby took a deep breath, trying as hard as she could to hold back the tears that threatened to stream down her face. "Over and over you've told me that there is nothing between you and Sherry. That you're just friends. Then I hear the Sheriff nonchalantly joking that she's in your office so much she might as well be your secretary?"

"Shelby, I didn't do anything. I swear I haven't done anything,"Todd said defensively and firmly. "God, they were just kidding around because they heard what happened at the party. No one can say anything or do anything without you jumping to conclusions can they?"

Shelby sat back in her seat and turned to look out the window as she nervously bit on her lower lip. She could feel her strength dissolving. Her resolve to finally stand up for herself and to express her anger instead of meekly swallowing it was quickly fading. She had moments earlier been so sure that Todd couldn't possibly weasel his way out this time and that she had finally caught him telling a bold face lie. Now she wasn't sure what to think.

Was she wrong? Was she completely off base like Todd always told her she was? Was all of this just a simple misunderstanding that she had blown completely out of proportion? Hadn't she finally decided to trust Todd completely and already she was wavering and allowing her insecurities to take over again?

As if by divine intervention, Shelby's questions were all answered for her when she got to work the next morning. After putting her purse in the nearby cabinet, she sat at her desk and systematically took the phones off of call forwarding where she had switched them the previous afternoon so the night dispatcher could take the incoming calls. Then she turned on her computer, when it came to life, there, in bold print was the name of the administrator who had logged into her computer sometime between when she'd left yesterday and just now.

Sherry Newman.

Dear God,

About this time of year, many years ago, I met a great guy who made me feel very special. Although I tried hard to convince myself that he was 'just another guy' I soon discovered that he had stolen my heart forever.

Throughout the years, I thought our love was genuine and pure. That we never played any games with each others hearts. I not only loved him, but I was always 'in love' with him. It wasn't what he did or didn't do, it was who he was and how he made me feel that made him special.

As I look back, I question whether my love for him was so blinding that I didn't see him slipping away. If I could have those months and years back, I'd show him how important he was to me.

I can't look to our future now, we live day by day. I don't know what is in his heart, I don't know what to do or say. I don't know how he feels about me, or whether his love is still true. I only hope and pray that in my life this man will stay and that our love will be renewed.

So, if by chance You see this man and he listens to what You say, tell him that I love him but head games I can no longer play. I'm trying to learn what pleases him, but I have needs too. A hug, a kiss, a kind word or two, would make my heart know the love we shared is still real and true. If this is too much bother and is too big a strain, I'm sorry but my heart can't take any more pain.

I need the guy that loved me, the one that really cared. The one who couldn't wait until the time when we'd be near. I think he's trying to find me, I can feel him near. But he's at the fork in the road and doesn't know which way to turn. He has to make a choice and it must be made clear, that whichever path he takes, the other will disappear. He needs Your help to make that choice so guide him if You can.

Amen –

* * *

Chapter Twenty

Shelby opened her eyes slowly and lifted her head from the back of the couch. Silent tears streaming down her cheeks but she beamed with a smile that was heartfelt and true. She was proud that she had been brave enough to finally stop listening to Todd's lies and acknowledged her gut instincts. She now felt light; the weight of the deceit Todd had burdened her with, finally lifted from her shoulders.

.   Discovering that half of her life had been lived in fallacy, was a shock to Shelby. Well, half of that half had been false anyway. Although Shelby now realized that her marriage had been a sham, she also realized that the part of her life that was the most important to her was honest and true. Her love for her children could never be taken from her. They had been the focus of her life and were her absolute pride and joy. She had jobs because financially she had needed to work. But they had only ever been jobs. Her career, her real passion in life, had been her children. How blessed she felt to have been their mom.

From that day on, Shelby had often wondered if there would be life after love. Days and weeks had run into months and still the hollowness, where her shattered heart had once beaten, remained heavy in her chest.

She grieved … not for the man who she was now divorced from, but for her marriage. She had poured every fiber of her being into that relationship; into the mindset that if she loved deeply and strongly enough, everything would be just fine.

She prayed … for guidance, for strength and for something that surprised her, for compassion.

She read … to calm and divert the attention of her racing thoughts. As she delved into the inspirational self-help books given to her by women who had also experienced her pain, she discovered what an enormous help they were. So she bought more of them. The words. The pain. These stories could have been written by her or about her. Somehow, it gave her strength to know that others had endured her pain and survived. Shelby wondered whether she could ever do or say something that would inspire another person to take off their rose-colored glasses, like the ones Todd had encouraged her to wear, so that they could see and deal with their relationship as it really was.

It wasn't until she ran into Rylee at a volleyball tournament, held outside the very same bowling alley that Shelby had worked at so many years before, that the uneasy feelings she had through the years about Todd were substantiated.

Rylee greeted her warmly and expressed her sympathy to Shelby about the break up of her marriage. Shelby felt foolish as her eyes began to yet again well up with tears, the pain still fresh and raw. Immediately, Rylee reached out and gently grasped Shelby's nervous hands that were tightly entwined, and held them in her own. She looked deeply and earnestly into Shelby's eyes and softly asked.

"You really don't know do you?"

"I don't know what?" Shelby asked in a hushed voice, filled with trepidation at what Rylee was about to tell her.

"You still sound so heartbroken about Todd having this affair," she said with concern, hesitating momentarily. "But, Todd has always had affairs."

Shelby didn't know what to do or say. She felt Rylee's hands gently gripping her arms as Rylee sat her slowly into the chair that stood empty beside them.

No, she didn't know. But it wasn't this shocking revelation that made her momentarily light headed. It was the miraculous discovery that she now knew for certain that she wasn't stupid, that she wasn't overly jealous, unreasonably suspicious or that her insecurities were unfounded. And most of all, she could dispel one of the most painful expressions Todd had used to waylay her uneasy feelings about him…

She wasn't crazy. And she never had been.

* * *

P.L. John

Sometimes the path life leads you on is straight
and smooth
Everywhere you look there are beautiful flowers
Breathtaking sunsets and a soft breeze at your back
And you're confident fate has pointed you in the right
direction.

Then all of a sudden there are wide curves in the road
And you seem to be going up and down hills
The flowers turn to weeds; the sunsets turn into gray skies
And the wind gusts towards you
Making it hard to continue on your journey.

You remember when the path was smooth
You know you haven't turned left or right
So you wonder why this path has changed course
And taken you so far from the land you once knew.

You persevere, believing that around the next bend
Your path will once again be as it was
But even though the path occasionally gets easier
You realize that it will never again be beautiful
and smooth.

When you feel you can't go any further
You look and a new path appears to your right
You can see a long way in the distance
Because the path is so straight and smooth.

You can see flowers off in the distance
And the sun seems to be shining brightly
You stand at the corner wondering
If you should take the new path or stay on the old.

You know that the old path was smooth
And beautiful for so many miles
You don't know whether to keep going
Or to believe that life is sending you on a new path.

You give that old path one more chance
But soon discover the path ends
Where you once walked has turned into a cliff
You know you can't go forward.

You're confused and disillusioned
And yet your dilemma isn't over
You need to decide whether to stand there by yourself
Or whether you should go down the other path.

Maybe the other path was an illusion
Maybe you needed some warmth
And beauty in your life again
So you imagined it was there.

Then you know that even if it wasn't there
The hope that it was there
Gave you the courage
To stand there by yourself instead of walking over the
cliff.

* * *

Epilogue

It had taken Shelby years to get completely through the grieving process. They had been unsettling years where she had struggled to understand what had happened and why she had allowed it. Todd may have taken advantage of her love for him, but she, like everyone else that played into his hands, had allowed it to happen.

Her heart was mending, her confidence and self-esteem returning, her mind clearing and her eyes opening to the truth and realities of life and love. Shelby's enthusiasm for life had returned and she was eager to see what kind of adventure this next phase of her life would bring.

At hearing the doorbell ring, Charlie instantly began to bark as he ran towards the door preparing to defend his domain. Shelby smiled wistfully. Even if by chance she hadn't heard the doorbell ring, her dogs attentive barks were enough to alert her that someone was at the door.

As she walked out of her bedroom to answer the door, Shelby primped her hair, adjusted her mid-length sundress and tried to ease the giddy nervousness that had been building up in her the entire afternoon.

It had taken her time to recover from the emotional turmoil she experienced while opening her heart and memory to the sad reality of her marriage to Todd, but she was now ready to move forward in every aspect of her life.

When she peaked out of the curtained window of the door, her face broke into a warm smile. Charlie likewise stopped his barking and began wildly wagging his tail and whining at the recognition of the familiar friendly face.

Shelby opened the door to welcome Ron inside and as she did, Charlie ran past her and jumped on him excitedly in anticipation of the treat he always brought. For a second, Shelby wondered whether she should be more earnest about teaching the dog not to jump on people. That worry quickly dissipated when Ron began to laugh heartily at the dog's exuberance. Shelby broke out laughing too.

After patting Charlie affectionately, Ron gave him the dog bone he had taken out of his blazer pocket. As the beagle happily padded his way back into the cozy apartment, Ron brought his left arm out from behind his back.

Shelby gasped when she saw that he was holding a bouquet of spring daisies and tulips.

"Oh, Ron. They're beautiful," Shelby sighed as she reached for the aromatic bouquet.

"Beautiful flowers for my beautiful lady," Ron said softly as his deep blue eyes gazed at her lovingly.

* * *

Coming Soon

Choosing Her Next Path
The beginning of a journey towards faith

by

P. L. John

* * *

Made in the USA
Lexington, KY
14 January 2010